LOVE MATCH

I had seen him from a distance earlier, volleying on the boys' court, and had noticed that besides being a pretty good tennis player, he was incredibly good-looking.

Now I looked up and met his gaze. He stared back at me with intense blue eyes, creased slightly against the brightness of the sun and made even more blue by his tan.

Suddenly, everything happened just as it does in corny old movies—my heart beat fast, bells started ringing, birds started singing, the whole world spun around at double speed.

It was a classic case of love at first sight . . .

LOVE MATCH

Janet Quin-Harkin

BANTAM BOOKS
TORONTO · NEW YORK · LONDON · SYDNEY

RL 6, IL age 11 and up

LOVE MATCH

A Bantam Book/February 1982

Sweet Dreams is a Trademark of Bantam Books, Inc.

ISBN 0-553-20745-8

Published simultaneously in the United States and Canada

PRINTED IN THE UNITED STATES OF AMERICA

0 9 8 7 6 5 4 3

For Elizabeth St. Davids Schiffman,
Writer, tennis player and friend.

Chapter One

I sat on the bench in the treehouse, catching my breath from the climb up the tree. The late March New England air was chilly, and although my down jacket felt bulky, I was glad I had worn it.

Years before, when my brothers had built the treehouse, I had nailed pieces of wood to the trunk to use as steps. But over the years they had rotted and crumbled, and I didn't trust them. So I had climbed the tree the hard way, finding toeholds in the bark and pulling myself up by my arms from branch to branch. It was the same way I had climbed the tree the first time, when I was eight.

We had just moved to the house we still live in. My father had been offered the head coach's job at the college here. I was the only one in my family who had not been thrilled for him and happy to move. I didn't want to leave my friends in Boston and move to the country, where I was sure I would die of boredom. I remember that I sulked and raged and actually packed my bags several times to run away from home.

When the moving truck was ready to go, I hid in my favorite spot under the basement steps and listened as my parents and three brothers rushed through the house, enticing and threatening me to "come out, come out, wherever you are." To tell the truth, I was getting worried that they'd give up and drive away, leaving me in an empty house. But of course they finally found me. And I sulked for the whole two-hundred-mile trip to our new home.

While the others oohed and aahed over the big old house with its sloping ceilings and attic bedrooms, I sat on the front porch and pouted. Just before it got dark, I noticed one apple tree that towered above the others in the orchard that partially surrounded the house. It was just begging to be climbed, and I hurried off to climb it. But when I stood at its foot and saw how big it really was, I didn't feel quite so brave. The trunk was so thick that I couldn't reach around it, and its first branch was way above my head. Still, I never was the sort of child to chicken out on something I had dared myself to do. I scrambled up, ripping my good pants and skinning one knee, which was already covered with the scars of past mishaps.

I climbed up and up then, not caring that the ground seemed awfully far away and that the branches were swaying in the strong wind. At last I came to the perfect place—two wide branches extending like open arms from the trunk; I knew it would be just right for a treehouse. Once I was settled with my legs astride one of the branches, I realized that my perfect place had an added bonus—a view of the road below as it wound all the way down the hill to the narrow iron bridge. It was an ideal place for a spy, and at that time spying was one of the careers I was considering.

The old house was big and welcoming, and after a few days I felt as if we had never lived anywhere else. My family immediately fell into their old routines—my oldest brother, Greg, the tennis freak, disappearing with his tennis racket at dawn; Peter, the physical fitness freak, going off jogging through the local woods; and Martin, who was only a year older than me, throwing a ball endlessly against the garage wall. I was determined to have my treehouse built as soon as possible, and they were equally determined that my treehouse was not going to interfere with their training schedules.

In the end I had to resort to some persuasive threats and even tantrums to get them to come and help me. Finally they all decided that building a treehouse was much simpler and less painful than being bugged all day by a whining sister, and it was finished in a couple of weeks.

Now, seven years later, it looked just as it always had—which was a tribute to my brothers' good workmanship and my slave driving.

I hadn't been in the treehouse since last summer, when I had come up here with the girls who I had thought were my friends, and we had had a big argument. After that, I hadn't gone back to the treehouse because I didn't want to be reminded of that awful day. Yet, it was still my secret hiding place, and I had returned to it now as a last refuge, as a place to think.

"This is my sophomore year," I said aloud, "and I should be enjoying myself. I had fun in grade school. Even partway through junior high. I used to have lots of friends. What's happened to me?"

I knew the answer, of course. I hadn't changed, and they had. That was obvious. Angela, my former best friend of the tree-house days, now wore thick eye makeup and spent hours in front of her mirror every morning with her hot comb, making sure her hair was flipped just right. Dee Dee, who had been so skinny that we always had chosen her to creep under fences and retrieve lost balls, had curves that were the envy of every girl in the class and got long looks from every boy. Weird Shelly, who most of the kids wouldn't play with because she dressed in black and said strange things, had turned into a horribly normal teenager who wore jeans with the right label on them and squeaked, "He's so cute!" about every boy she saw. Even homely Martha, who used to calm us down when we got excited, warn us about dangers when we wanted to do something crazy, and made peace when we fought, had lost about fifty pounds and could be heard giggling hysterically and loudly all the way across the cafeteria.

I was the only one who hadn't changed. My mind just didn't work like Angela's or Dee Dee's anymore. I couldn't see any sense in spending hours working on my hair when it just hung like a limp mop. There was no point in putting on nail polish when it only chipped as soon as I picked up a tennis racket. And to be very honest, I preferred to spend my clothing allowance on one cheap pair of jeans and some good tennis shoes rather than on designer jeans. It didn't matter to me what the label on my bottom said.

There was something definitely wrong with me, and I didn't know how to go about making it right. . . .

Chapter Two

I suppose it all came down to being a late bloomer. That was what my mother called me, at any rate, but she was only trying to make me feel better. I don't know why I couldn't get all excited about boys, the way other girls could. It wasn't that I was shy. Someone with three older brothers, their friends, and an entire college football team hanging around the house could hardly grow up shy with boys. It was just that boys were something I took for granted. I couldn't see anything special in them.

It took me about the first eight years of my life to realize that I wasn't a boy myself. I did everything my brothers did—I wrestled and kicked and tore my jeans and got in trouble just like they did.

Right after we moved to this house, my brother Martin told the kids in my new class that there were only three things worth knowing about me: one, I could throw a ball as hard as any boy; two, I knew over two hundred elephant jokes; and three, I had a terrible temper.

I was furious that he had dared to say such awful things about me to complete strangers, who would now never like me, and I demonstrated both my temper and my strength by kicking Martin so hard I made him cry.

But when I actually arrived at the new school, I discovered that my brother's description of me had had the opposite effect. The kids gave me a great welcome and looked at me with respect. After all, it is not every kid who knows that many elephant jokes and can throw a ball. Also, I guess I looked tough enough to beat them to a pulp if they didn't laugh at my joke about the elephant in the refrigerator.

Even Scott McKinley, the toughest boy in the third grade, had to grudgingly admit that I could throw a football harder than he could, and he invited me to become a member of his gang.

When I accepted a dare to walk along a ledge above the school front door, which nobody else had ever dared to cross, my stock rose even higher. In fact, my entry into third grade was the high point of my life. All the third graders, including Scott McKinley and his gang, looked up to me as a hero. I had reached the peak of my career at the age of eight, and since then, things had been going steadily downhill.

I was jarred back from my thoughts by some sounds below me. A group of kids was walking up the street from the bridge. Before I could see them, I heard the high voices and loud giggles. When the five girls came into view, my heart gave a lurch as if I were seeing a vision or a ghost. For a moment I almost thought it was me coming up the hill with the other members of the treehouse gang, just as we had always walked home from school. And suddenly the days of the Treehouse Five seemed like yesterday and not years ago. . . .

Scott McKinley and I became big buddies— joint leaders of the third grade. "De Mayo, come over and look at this," he would yell, calling me by my last name, the way all the tough boys in school talked to one another. He would ask my opinion on everything important, like who to pick for our football team.

In those days I didn't have much time for girls. I tended to agree with Scott that they were a boring and wishy-washy bunch of creatures who cried when they fell down and squealed if an ant climbed on them. Angie, our neighbor across the street, was a good example.

"Why don't you play with Angela?" my parents were always suggesting, while I vowed that nothing in this world would make me play with Angela. She was the kind of little girl who never got dirty and who wore frilly dresses and ribbons in her hair. Ever since the ledge-walking episode, I was her big hero. She and her friends used to follow me around, waiting for me to notice them. They used to come by in the morning and walk me to school, fight to sit next to me at lunch, and stare in wonder when Scott called me over to have a conference. I thought they were all boring because none of them knew how to play football.

That year, I had decided what my career was going to be. I was going to be a professional football player. Nobody in my family had mentioned that football was not meant for girls. At school I was as good as Scott was. So when he went along to try out for the Pop Warner team, I went along, too. The coach took one look at me and laughed.

"What are you doing here?" he asked. "Run along home now."

"I'm here to try out for the team," I said.

"Not my team, you're not," said the coach,

and he wouldn't listen to any of my pleas.

I ran all the way home, expecting my family to back me up, but instead they all laughed.

"Boy, what a dummy," Martin said. "You ought to know they don't allow girls to play football."

"But I'm as good as the boys! It's not fair," I wailed.

"But, honey, it's no big deal," soothed my mother. "After all, you're good at lots of other sports."

"Yeah, if you keep practicing with me, I'll make a tennis player of you," said my big brother, Greg, who had just won a tennis scholarship to college. But at that time I didn't want to be a tennis player. I wanted to be a football player. It seemed like the end of the world.

My relationship with Scott changed, too. All his gang had made the football team, so they didn't have much time for me. And I came to the bitter realization that I was a girl, after all—however much I wanted to be a boy.

It was at that stage that I began to take more interest in Angie and her friends—Dee Dee the Shrimp, Martha the Chubby, and Shelly the Weird. They were thrilled that I finally wanted to play with them, and I was amazed to find they were not nearly as boring as I had thought. We spent a wonderful summer up in my treehouse. And they watched admiringly while I tried out one stunt more daring than the last on my new trapeze, which Greg had built for me as a going-away-to-college present.

By the end of the summer I had shaped up my four followers into a pretty neat bunch of kids. They no longer screamed when ants crawled over them, and Dee Dee could walk along the longest branch without holding on. Because Angela lived so close, she and I became sort of best friends, spending long hours in the evening walking her dog or just sitting around and talking.

Then the following year something happened to change my whole outlook on life. Greg made an unexpected trip home from college to announce that he was going to quit school and become a professional tennis player. My parents weren't too happy about this, but they finally gave a grudging okay. To me, it was the most exciting thing I had ever heard.

"Are you really going to get paid for playing tennis?" I asked in wonder.

"Only if I win," he said.

I went away to think about it.

"Imagine," I said to the gang in the treehouse. "Imagine getting paid for traveling around the world and playing tennis. That's the neatest thing I ever heard of. That's just what I'll be—a tennis player."

I thought the others would be impressed. But they weren't.

"I wouldn't want to be traveling around all the time," Angie said. "That would mean leaving my husband and children."

"I'm going to be a nurse," said Dee Dee. "Or maybe a teacher."

"Me, too," said Martha.

"I should think you'd get awful tired of playing tennis all the time," Shelly said.

I looked from one to the other. It was the first time they had not thought that what I did was fantastic. I should have realized then that we were different.

Every summer after that, I started doing what Greg had done; I went out with my tennis racket after breakfast and practiced hard all morning. I hung around the local courts and would play with anybody who would have me. When there was no one to play with, I used to knock the ball against the training wall for hours. And I got better and better. I loved it.

My treehouse friends complained that they hardly ever saw me. But when we did meet in the treehouse, we still had a lot of fun. By now, we were eleven, and we giggled a lot. We invented a secret treehouse club with all sorts of rules and a proper chairman (me) and secretary (Angie). We had a little red-covered notebook in which we kept secrets about people at school or people we spied on as they walked below our tree.

Remembering the little red book now, I got down on my knees on the treehouse floor to see if it was still there. We had made a secret compartment for it, under the bench. I touched a couple of cobwebs, but then my fingers felt it, and I pulled the book out. The red cover had faded, coloring the first pages red, but the writing was still quite legible— Angie's neat, slanting, one-hundred-percent-correct handwriting, my uneven scrawl, and the others'. It was a history of two years in the treehouse club.

THE TREEHOUSE FIVE. TOP SECRET. DO NOT OPEN OR PROCEED ON PAIN OF DEATH was written on the first page by me. The pages were filled with observations about ourselves and those around us. "Mrs. Silver wears false teeth. Dee Dee saw her take them out. Martin de M. used a four-letter word while walking under our tree and talking to Danny P. Peter de M. kissed Michele at the school dance. Artie cheated on the history test—he had the dates written on a little piece of paper up his sleeve."

These had all been terribly important secrets at the time, and they seemed so small now. Had we really wasted all that time and energy spying on people to uncover such stupid facts about them? And yet I remember how we grabbed each other's arms in the hall and whispered together. "I just got another secret," we would hiss, then run giggling into the bathroom to confide it.

Page after page of outgrown secrets taking us right through sixth grade and seventh, now all molding and faded. Then my eye was caught by Dee Dee's backward-slanting handwriting. It was a transition secret, a hint of things to come. "Scott McKinley likes Angie." I had laughed at it at the time.

Chapter Three

It was the summer after ninth grade that marked the start of my misery. Things were happening that I couldn't control. Everybody was growing up and changing into someone I no longer knew. I felt as if I were on an escalator that was taking me away from my safe, secure world—from the world where Scott McKinley used to yell, "Hey, de Mayo! Get over here!" And however fast I ran to get back to the bottom of that escalator, it was never fast enough.

On the surface, nothing much had changed in ninth grade. Our last year in junior high was pretty much the same as the other two. The girls still came by in the morning, and we walked home in the afternoon and met in the treehouse on good days. But they no longer met to be part of the treehouse gang, and they no longer looked on me as their leader. I might have been pretty naive, but I was not too stupid to realize why they kept coming to my treehouse. They came there to spy on and talk about boys.

I put up with it because, after all, they still came and were still my friends, even if they did talk about eye shadow and cute boys and made fun of my constant tennis practice. And anyway, it was better than having no friends at all.

But I was beginning to get very fed up with the whole thing. Their stupid conversations and giggling annoyed me even more because secretly I was worried that I wasn't interested in the same things they were. I didn't think eye shadow was important, and I didn't think that boys were worth spying on, and it didn't make me go all weak at the knees when the ninth-grade heartthrob sat next to me for lunch.

"What's the matter with me?" I asked my mother. "Everyone else seems to have moved to a different planet except me. They're all talking about boys all the time, and I think all the boys in my class are jerks. Is there something wrong with them or me?"

My mother laughed. "There's nothing wrong with any of you, silly. You are just maturing at a different pace, that's all. You want to hang on to being a little girl for a while longer—and that's not such a bad thing, either. But you'll grow up in the end."

"You mean I'll start acting like that when boys are around? Is that growing up?"

"Part of it. After all, if men and women didn't begin to find each other attractive as they grew up, no one would ever marry and produce the next generation, would they?"

I had to laugh. "But I can't ever imagine myself feeling all dizzy because some boy says hi to me. Do you suppose that means I'll never get married?"

My mother smiled a sort of secret smile. "You wait, my girl. One day you'll meet a special boy, and it will happen so fast you'll wonder what hit you."

That was hard for me to believe. I thought every boy was a creep, and I was sick of hearing my former best friends talk about them.

I suppose it was inevitable that it should all explode into a great fight one day. We were all ripe for it—getting on one another's nerves when we sat in the treehouse with no boys to watch.

It was extra hot, even for August. The road below us had disappeared into a shimmering heat haze, and the grass below the apple tree was burned golden brown. For the past few days it had been too hot to do anything. I had been getting up at six to practice tennis—spurred on by the fact that my professional tennis star brother was home for a couple of weeks and was willing to hit the ball around with his little sister. His play had improved incredibly, and my right shoulder ached all day from the jarring it got trying to return his serves. But I loved every minute of it.

By eight or so it was too hot to go on playing, which was a good thing, because my body would not stand up to more tennis with Greg than that.

I hadn't seen too much of the other girls since school had let out. They all had other things to do. Angela was an assistant counselor at a kids' day camp, Dee Dee was on a swim team, Shelly was writing the great American novel, and Martha was helping her folks in the family store. But one hot Saturday afternoon they all came back to the treehouse where it was cool and you could feel the breeze from the river.

"It's been the most boring summer ever." Angie sighed as she lay on her stomach on the pillows, wearing a tiny bright-pink bikini. "Those little kids are such monsters. I'm sure we were never like that when we were their age."

"Yes, we were," I reminded her. "We used to

have our *circus* and drop on people from the trapeze as they walked under the tree."

"*You* did," said Angie in a bored voice. "I never went in for that sort of childish stuff."

There was an icy silence.

"Hey, Joanna," Shelly said at last. "Where are your brothers today?"

I didn't answer. All of a sudden the truth hit me: it was not the heat that had brought the girls to my treehouse, it was my good-looking brothers. That shows you how dumb I was. I began to feel angry and hurt. These girls didn't care at all about me—they just wanted to see my brothers.

I looked from one to the other. What had happened to my former friends, to my Treehouse Five, who would have followed me to the ends of the earth, who rolled around laughing at my elephant jokes and laughed even more at my mad practical jokes? Angie had been lying. They had joined in when I jumped down to scare people walking under the tree. I could remember her peering down from the branches and whispering, "Here he comes now! Go on, jump!"

Now we never laughed together. I longed for those crazy times again. Perhaps it was because I didn't play jokes anymore. Perhaps a joke was just what we needed to start us all laughing again.

Then I had a great idea. I had brought up a large pitcher of Kool-Aid. The others were lounging about half asleep. I leaned across and picked up the pitcher. Then I swung out of the treehouse and climbed to the branch above. I sat there for a moment, watching the girls through the slats in the roof. Angie's bare back was right below me.

"Hey, Angie," I called. "Guess what?"

She looked up, trying to figure out where my voice was coming from.

"It's raining!" I yelled and tipped the Kool-Aid over her.

I didn't think she would mind getting wet. After all, it was hot, wasn't it? But she leaped to her feet, her mouth open in a sort of silent scream. I waited for the others to burst into hysterical laughter, but there was only silence.

At last Angie found her voice. "Oh, you idiot!" she screamed. "Just look what you've done!"

"You and your dumb jokes, Joanna," said Martha. "Here, Angie, take my towel."

"A towel's no good, I'm all sticky," Angie sobbed. "I'll have to run home and shower. Oh, I hope no one sees me. With my luck I'll bump into Scott looking like this."

"I'll walk you home," Martha said.

"How could you do a thing like that, Joanna?" Dee Dee said.

21

"It was a joke," I said. "I didn't think anyone would mind getting wet when they were wearing a bikini on a hot day—"

"Some joke," snapped Angie.

"But you've ruined her hair," said Dee Dee, as if she were talking to a child. "Didn't you remember that she's going to the dance tonight at the church youth group? Now she'll have to wash her hair and set it again."

"OK. I'm sorry," I said. They were all starting to climb down.

"You should be." Angie's eyes blazed up at me with hatred. "It's about time you grew up a bit, Joanna de Mayo. You're too old to still be acting like a tomboy. You won't catch me coming to your dumb treehouse again, even to see Greg!"

Then my temper took over. "Don't worry. I wouldn't want you in my treehouse," I yelled after them. "You've all turned into a bunch of boring jerks. . . . Oh, Greg, you're sooo cute. . . . That's all you think about—boys, boys, boys!"

They never came back to the treehouse. That was last summer, and I could still remember the pain and anger I felt as they walked away.

I stirred uneasily on the hard treehouse bench; I wished I had not come up here again.

When we all started tenth grade last September, the only person I could still come close to calling a friend was Dee Dee. Whenever Angela and I were forced together, she managed to ignore me completely, and we didn't speak to each other at all for a couple of months. Dee Dee still invited me to her slumber parties or to sit with them in the cafeteria or to go to football and basketball games, but lately I had begun to make excuses not to go. I had a feeling Dee Dee only felt sorry for me and that the others were complaining about her dragging me along. After all, why bother? We had nothing in common, since I couldn't share their gossip about boys and dates, and whenever I talked about tennis, they'd patronize me for a while and then dismiss me as some backward child.

True, I had developed a passable figure and grown quite tall and had nice straight teeth now that the braces had finally been removed. But I still didn't have a boyfriend and, quite frankly, there was no boy I wanted for a boyfriend.

There had been one occasion during the last year when I wondered if I was growing into a normal, mature woman-to-be after all. That was when I bumped into my old buddy, Scott McKinley. We came toward each other in the narrow hall to the gymnasium. Every time I saw him I was surprised at how he was changing from a scruffy, skinny little freckle-covered kid into a tall, muscular boy.

"Hey, de Mayo!" he said, and I noticed that his voice was becoming smooth and deep. But when his face broke into a grin, he still looked like my old friend again. "Long time, no see. How ya been?"

"OK, I guess," I said, feeling suddenly tongue-tied and starting to blush.

"You still play football?" he asked, and I could tell he was teasing me.

"No, but I see you do," I said. "Congratulations on making the team."

He grinned again. "Yeah! How about that. Only sophomore to make it. I owe some of that to your coaching—after all, you taught me to pass."

I tried to find an answer, but none would come. I wasn't sure if he was making fun of me or not.

"I saw your brother on TV last week," Scott went on. "He must be making a lot of money. He'll be a millionaire soon."

I laughed. "I wish. He has to pay a lot of expenses to be on tour, you know—plane tickets and hotel bills, and if he doesn't win, he doesn't get paid. When he starts winning the big tournaments, I guess he'll be rich, but up to now he's never managed better than fourth, and that only pays a few thousand. Usually he's been unlucky and drawn people like John McEnroe in the first round."

As if in silent agreement, we started to walk side by side down the hall to the gym. For a while neither of us spoke.

"And how's your tennis going?" Scott finally asked. It was a question I hadn't been expecting. It threw me off balance for a minute. I didn't think anyone around here knew or cared about my tennis. After all, I seldom talked about it. I had a secret goal, actually, of practicing on my own and then emerging one day as a great champion. So no one in high school had ever seen me play. I had deliberately steered clear of the local championships. I wanted to wait until I felt I was good enough. I was realistic enough to recognize that I was not yet another Greg. Perhaps if I could get some good coaching one day and some good competition . . .

"My tennis?" I repeated. "Oh, it's coming along pretty slowly at the moment. I need some decent coaching. Greg helps me when he's home, but he's never home these days."

"Join the tennis team then," Scott said.

"I plan to," I said, but I sighed inwardly. I had watched the girls' tennis coach in action. She was also the girls' volleyball coach and gymnastics coach, and she knew a little about all three, but not much about any one. In our part of the country, they were not too hot on girls' sports, and our sports budget was enough to buy one volleyball per season.

We reached the gymnasium, and Scott held open the door for me.

"Hey, Scottie," called a voice behind us, and Artie, the former child creep, came running toward us. Scott stopped and waited for him. "Where've you been?" Artie said. "I've been waiting for you for hours."

"I've just been having a little talk," Scott said, looking at me.

Artie noticed me for the first time. "You better not let Angie see you with another girl," he said, grinning in my direction. "You know she's the jealous type."

"This isn't another girl," Scott said. "It's only de Mayo."

Artie's face lit up as he recognized me. "Oh, yeah. You still play football?" he asked, giving me a stupid grin.

I shook my head and turned away. "I'd better hurry, I'm late for P.E.," I said, and disappeared into the darkness of the gymnasium. I felt like a balloon that had been pricked. I wasn't another girl, a girl who could be a threat to somebody's boyfriend. I was only de Mayo, someone who had once played football.

It was a hurt that wouldn't go away. After school that night I studied myself carefully in the bedroom mirror. Was I really so different from other girls? Did I look like a boy? Like an old witch? My face looked back at me—it wasn't a bad face at all. Sort of roundish with a big wide grin when I smiled (which wasn't often anymore). I didn't wear makeup because I couldn't be bothered, but looking at my complexion I decided that I didn't need to. My skin was darkish and gave the impression of a healthy tan. I supposed my eyebrows needed shaping, but I hated the agony of plucking them. Then my hair—well, my hair was sort of blah, pulled straight back and held with a rubber band. But it wasn't ugly hair—not stringy and dirty and lifeless. It was a good blackish-brown color, and it was nice and thick.

The rest of me was tall but not unnaturally tall—around five-foot-five—and my bones were sturdy but not too big for a girl. And I did have a bust and a waist and hips. So why did they all think of me as "only de Mayo"?

I suppose I have an image I have to live

down, I thought. I had wanted them to think of me as one of the boys—and now they did.

As I studied myself further, it was clear that my image was not improved by what I was wearing. My jeans were plain blue Levi's and were not molded to me like those that most girls wore. My top was Greg's old UCLA sweatshirt. Hardly sexy. But I didn't want to look sexy, did I? The trouble was that I didn't know what I wanted.

But I do know that I experienced my first stab of jealousy right after that meeting with Scott. I knew that he and Angie had had a couple of dates, but I couldn't believe he could actually take her seriously. After all, the Scott I used to know liked practical girls who knew about football, not the helpless type that Angie had turned into.

But then, I bumped into them one day as I was coming out of algebra. They were holding hands and walking very close together. Scott mumbled a slightly embarrassed hi when he saw me, but Angie purred, "Oh, hi, Jo-ann-a," like a contented lioness. I sort of nodded in their direction and walked on. As I passed she turned to whisper something to him, and they both laughed. I didn't know if it was about me. But the thought did stab into me: why her? What's wrong with my old friend Scott that he would fall for a girl like that?

A cold breeze began to blow through the treehouse, and I realized I'd been there for over two hours. Time to go down and face reality, I thought. Easter vacation was over, and it was back to school the next day. Back to being nobody—lost among a thousand students. Back to being "only de Mayo." Next week there were tryouts for the tennis team, but I didn't see how they could change anything.

Chapter Four

Growing up in a family like mine, you don't get too nervous about playing sports. I had watched my father's football teams in important playoffs. I had watched Greg playing Jimmy Connors. I had watched Peter stumbling through six-mile cross-country races, and Martin swaggering out to bat. Sports were a major part of our lives, so we took them pretty much for granted. True, there was a thrill of excitement when Dad's star running back made the impossible touchdown and when Greg took a set from Connors, but it was a nice sort of excitement—the sort of thing you talk about at the dinner table afterward. "Wasn't it exciting when. . . ." "Yes, but how about the time that . . ."

I was the only one in the family who still had to prove myself in sports. Even my mother, whose only sports activity these days was golf, had once held the junior state high-jump record. Looking at her now, petite compared to her husky family, it was hard to imagine her as an athlete, but she had the cup in the trophy closet to prove it, while I still had nothing.

Nobody who mattered had watched me play tennis yet. Greg had told me that I was beginning to shape up, and I was considered pretty good at my parents' club, where I played occasionally, but there I played mostly against weekend players who weren't too serious about their games. So, quite frankly, when I went down for the tennis team tryouts, I had no idea how good I was. I was more nervous than any de Mayo ought to have been.

Our school had two sets of tennis courts: the old ones, with bits of grass growing out of the cracks and with trees looming overhead that shed odd seeds and leaves at various seasons; and four beautiful new ones with handsome red playing surfaces. It didn't take a genius to figure out which courts the girls' team got.

There were quite a few girls on the courts when I arrived, and I tried to look cool, swinging my racket in one hand to show how relaxed I was. No one noticed my arrival, which was a good thing since I had just miscalculated my swing and brought the racket down on my ankle by mistake. So I stood in the shade at the edge of the group and studied the clouds racing over the hill.

"I don't recognize you. Is this the first time you've tried out?" asked a voice beside me. It took me a moment to realize that the girl was talking to me. I turned around to see a very sophisticated-looking girl, perfectly made up, her hair in place, and wearing a pretty, frilly tennis skirt. She was also wearing brand-new, baby-blue Nikes. The girls standing next to her all looked pretty much the same—like fashion models. I began to feel like a kindergarten kid who had wandered into the wrong schoolyard.

"I asked if this is the first time you've tried out?" the girl repeated kindly.

I nodded. "That's right," I mumbled.

"Are you a sophomore then?"

I nodded again. She had obviously dismissed me from her mind as someone hopelessly boring. She gave me a half-hearted sort of smile. "Well, good luck then. I hope you make it." Then she turned back to her friends. With nothing else to do, I listened to their conversation.

"So it will probably be you and Jackie who play the singles this year, and Kim and I will be the doubles."

"Unless there's any new talent."

"Doesn't look like any. I've never seen most of these kids before. They didn't play in the Hartford tournament last month."

"Oh, I meant to ask you about that. How did it go?"

"Not bad. I was third in the singles. The two winners were both ranked players, so I didn't feel too bad."

"Hey, that's good, Jackie. I wanted to enter, but we were in Florida that week."

I began to sink into gloom. What if I didn't even make the tennis team? How could I ever face my family? My tennis was the only thing I had going for me, the only goal I had in life, the only thing that I really loved. What would I do if I never made it as a tennis player?

At that moment I longed to be eight years old again, for I was full of confidence then— too full of confidence, in fact. I was like an eight-year-old Muhammad Ali—I was the greatest, and I knew it. "I'll pitch," I'd say when we played baseball at school. "I'll be quarterback. I can pass best," when we played football. And they always let me be what I wanted because I was the best.

But now I didn't seem to be best at anything. What if the tennis coach watched me play, then said, "Nice try, honey. Come back next year"?

My thoughts were interrupted by the arrival of Miss Howard, the coach. She was an energetic, pretty, older woman, who had taught physical education for years and was made the girls' tennis team coach because the school couldn't afford to hire anybody else.

"All right, ladies, gather round," she said. Jackie and her friends strolled toward her. The rest of us shuffled after them.

"I'm going to divide you into fours, and I want you to warm up for about ten minutes on the courts," Miss Howard said. "Why don't you four take court one?"

She pointed to me and the three nearest me. We didn't look at each other as we went onto court one, luckily the least grassy and cracked of the two. I walked around the net. The girl opposite me gave me a weak sort of smile.

"I'm hopeless," she said. "I didn't want to try out for the team at all, but my mother kept at me. She's the star of the tennis club."

"That's bad luck," I agreed and thought how funny it was that my family, who were at the top in the world of sports, didn't make me do anything. Was that a good or a bad thing? It meant either that they didn't care about what I did—which I didn't really believe—or that if I made it and achieved something, I'd know I made it on my own. I decided my family's way was better.

Then Miss Howard opened a can of balls and handed them to the girl who claimed to be hopeless. She promptly served it into the net. The next one sailed over my head, and the third went right over the fence of the court. She was right; she was hopeless. I felt sorry for her and gave her a nice, low, gentle shot to return. She rushed forward, swung at it, and missed completely.

Now I was in a dilemma. I felt sorry for the girl, it was true, but I didn't want to be included in her hopelessness. I didn't want Miss Howard to say, "Oh, you four are no good. Let's try another four." So I sent one across court to the other girl. She returned it, and I sent it back again just as Miss Howard came in our direction. We continued with a cross-court game for a few minutes until Miss Howard stopped us.

"Jackie," she called, "I think I'm going to need you after all. Would you come over here and play against this young lady for a while?" She turned to me. "What's your name, dear?"

I told her. "Play against Joanna here, will you, Jackie?" she said. Jackie gave her a confident nod.

We hit the ball back and forth for a few minutes. She was good, but I had a feeling she was working herself much harder than I was. I was doing what Greg had told me to.

"Never give any secrets away in your warm-up," he'd always said. "Just return the ball and don't hit hard. That way you can see what they are like and then take them by surprise."

Miss Howard nodded in satisfaction. "All right, ladies. How about playing a few games?" She handed the balls to me to serve.

I served hard and straight down the center line. Jackie didn't even bother to move, so I assumed it must have been out. I went to serve again, but Miss Howard called, "Fifteen-love." So I walked to the left side. Jackie was frowning. I wondered if she didn't agree with the call. But when I served again, she didn't touch my second serve, either, nor the third, and she only managed to tip my fourth, sending the ball crazily up into the air. "Game," Miss Howard called.

Jackie shot me a look that was pure daggers as I handed her the balls to serve. I knew how she felt; after all, pretty much the same thing happened to me when I played against Greg. Usually I couldn't return his serves. But I tried harder than she did!

I didn't have to do much to win the second

game either and Miss Howard stopped us before I could serve again.

"Just wait there for a minute, will you, ladies? I see Mr. Parker over there, and I want a word with him. I'll be right back." She trotted off to talk to a man on the boys' court.

Jackie strolled back to her friends, and I joined the other kids at the side of the court.

"Who's Mr. Parker?" I asked the girl beside me.

"He's the coach for the boys' team," she said. Then she leaned closer to me and grinned. "Boy, you sure were giving Jackie a whipping. I bet she never forgives you for that. She thinks she's the hot-shot around here."

"She does?"

"Yeah, she was one of the two singles players last year. Now the other girl has gone on to college, and she expects to be number one this year."

My heart gave an excited little leap. Was I really that much better than the number one? Was I really going to be like the rest of my family, after all—to be able to announce at dinner, "I'm the best girl tennis player in the school"?

Then Miss Howard appeared with a red-faced, jolly-looking man who could easily have doubled for Santa Claus if you put a red suit and a beard on him.

"OK, OK," he said, beaming at us all. "Now where's the eighth wonder of the world I've got to watch in action?"

Miss Howard turned to me, then looked across to Jackie. "Jackie, would you play with Joanna again for us?" she asked.

Jackie's face turned bright crimson, and I couldn't tell whether it was from rage or embarrassment. "No, thanks," she said and turned her back on me.

We all stood around in silence. I felt everybody's eyes on me and wished that the ground would swallow me up.

"OK, OK," said Coach Parker at last, still trying to sound jolly. "I tell you what. You come with me, young lady, and I'll get you to play with one of my boys. Then we'll really see what sort of player you are."

As I followed him I was aware of the buzz of conversation that sprang up. Well, I wasn't a nobody now, that was one good thing. I'd made an impression on the girls' tennis team all right, but I wasn't sure it was a good one.

"What's your name?" Coach Parker asked as we walked to his set of courts. "Miss Howard was so excited that she didn't give me any details."

When I told him my name, his face lit up. "Ah, that explains everything. You're Greg de Mayo's little sister."

I nodded. He went on beaming at me as if I were a special birthday present he had just unwrapped. "I used to coach Greg when he was on the school team here. Did he ever mention me?"

I didn't want to offend him, so I said carefully, "I'm sure he must have talked about you at home, but I was kind of young when he was in high school. The people he talked about didn't mean anything to me then."

Coach Parker sighed. "He had so much talent, that boy. Of course, I helped him get his scholarship to UCLA. Haven't had anybody outstanding to coach since him. Let's see if you're going to follow in his footsteps, shall we?"

We reached the courts, and he opened the door for me with old-fashioned politeness. I stepped onto the smooth red surface.

"Now, let's find someone to play against you," he said, looking around hopefully as if he expected someone to materialize before him.

A boy in running clothes was jogging past. "Hey, David!"

"You want me?" the boy called back.

"I need one of my boys from the tennis team. Are any of them still hanging around the lockers? How about Tony?"

"No, he went home already. But Rick was still in the locker room."

"He'll do. Would you ask him to bring his racket and come out here for a few minutes?"

I waited, feeling very foolish as boys from various sports walked past toward their locker room and stared at me curiously. What was I doing on their tennis courts? the stares seemed to say. I pretended to be studying the gut on my racket and didn't look up until I heard the gate squeak closed.

"You wanted to see me, Coach?" asked a deep voice.

I had seen him from a distance earlier, volleying on the boys' court, and had noticed that besides being a pretty good tennis player, he was very good looking.

Now I looked up and met the boy's stare. He looked at me with incredibly blue eyes, made even more blue by his tan and by the blond hair that flopped into his eyes.

Suddenly everything happened just as my mother had said it would, just as in the corniest of old movies: my heart beat very fast, bells started ringing, birds started singing, the whole world spun around at double speed on its axis; it was a classic case of love at first sight. I'd waited fifteen years for this moment, and it was worth every second of waiting.

"Rick, this is Joanna de Mayo," Coach Parker said. "Joanna, this is Rick Hendricks. He's our number-one player this year."

"Hi," Rick said. But there was no expression in his voice, and his blue eyes did not smile.

I nodded, my feelings in a hopeless turmoil.

"So what did you want me for, Coach?" Rick went on as if I wasn't there. "I have to get home early. Got a heavy date tonight!" He grinned, showing his wonderful smile and making me feel insanely jealous of the girl who was going to get that smile directed at her tonight.

"I won't keep you long, Rick," Coach Parker said. "I just need you to play a couple of games with Joanna here. I want to see how she plays."

Rick's eyes narrowed. "You want me to play with *her*?" he said incredulously. "Why?"

"Coaches don't have to give reasons," Coach Parker said in a different voice, and I realized for the first time the strength beneath the jolly surface. "I just have to say, 'Get out there and play,' and you say, 'Yes, sir,' and do it. Is that clear?"

"Yes, sir," said Rick, giving a half grin and a

mock salute. He picked up a couple of balls and strolled down to the other end of the court.

"Here," he said and whammed one right at me. His wham was not nearly as hard as Greg's, so I sent it whizzing right back half an inch above the net and very fast. He stepped back in surprise and only managed a weak defensive shot back, which I finished off easily.

As the game went on, Rick frowned and pressed his lips together in a tight line. He was a good, consistent player, and he was pulling out every trick he knew. I was only amazed at how much harder I had to play against Greg.

After a few minutes the coach stopped us and called us over to him.

"That was great. Good play from both of you," he said.

Rick looked across at me. "You're pretty good," he said grudgingly, "for a girl."

"She'd be pretty good for a boys' team, too," Coach Parker said, "and you know it. She certainly made you work hard enough." He turned to me. "Joanna, you need more challenge than you'll get on the girls' team. You're not going to improve without some competition, and, quite frankly, my boys' team isn't too strong this year, apart from Rick here. So what do you say—can I persuade you to join my boys' team?"

Before I could answer, Rick spoke up. "Coach, you've got to be kidding! If she joins the team, I quit," he said and stomped off.

It was hardly a promising start to a romance.

Chapter Five

In spite of Rick's snub, I walked home on air. I thought about him all the way down River Street and nearly stepped out into traffic when the light was against me. I thought about him all the way up the hill, going over every detail of the way he looked: the way his hair flopped down into his eyes and how he tossed it back before he served; the way his eyes crinkled at the corners when he smiled; and the difference between his smile, which lit up his whole face and made his eyes sparkle, and the blank, icy expression he had given me.

That, of course, brought me down to earth with a bump. Whatever wonderful, dizzy, painful feelings were tingling through my body like electric shocks, it was pretty clear that I did nothing for Rick.

"Let's face it, Joanna," I said to myself as I walked up the last part of the hill, "you didn't actually expect a gorgeous boy like Rick to look twice at someone like you, did you?" Gloom began to settle on me as the hill got steeper and steeper. There really was no chance, was there? I couldn't have made a worse first impression. He was thrown off his guard at having to play me in the first place, and then I was every bit as good as he was—no wonder he didn't want me on his team.

After all, you don't get a boy to like you by humiliating him in front of his coach at his favorite sport, do you? I went over this again carefully in my mind. I hadn't really humiliated him, had I? He was a good player, and there were many times when I could have made him look bad by lobbing over his head or making a dropshot, and I didn't. I only gave him a good, hard game, and that's what any tennis player should want. Maybe he'd come around to seeing that. It might take a little time for him to accept me on the team, but once he saw I was an asset, he would accept me. And once he saw that I was a nice person as well, he might start liking me, maybe. . . .

After all, Coach Parker had been reassuring. "Don't pay any attention to him," he had said as Rick stomped away in a huff. "He's got a terrible temper. That's what makes him a good tennis player. He hates to be beaten! He'll be fine once he's cooled down."

I was still feeling the heartache of watching that departing back. "Perhaps I should quit and go back to the girls' team," I told the coach. "I really don't want to cause any trouble among your players. Maybe none of the other boys will want me, either."

"Nonsense," he said. "I'm the coach, and I say whom I want on the team. And if I say that King Kong is going to be their partner, they still play and don't argue. I think that you're the person this team needs this season, and I don't care if you're a girl, a boy, or a Martian. I need someone with your attacking drive. Rick will come around to seeing that. He's a sensible boy, apart from that temper."

"I ought to warn you right now that I have a bad temper, too. Or so my family always tells me," I said.

He laughed and covered his head with his hands. "Then heaven help me if the two of you get together."

I thought about those last words now as I turned into our gate. "If the two of you get together . . ." How sweet that sounded. I could imagine so clearly how that would be. Rick would come to accept me on the team, even admire me when I won some matches. Then one day our eyes would meet across the tennis court, maybe after I had scored the winning point, and he would know, as surely as I now knew, that we were meant for each other.

"Joanna and Rick," I said experimentally, "Rick and Joanna . . ."

"What are you muttering about?" asked Martin as I passed him in the front hall.

"Nothing," I said, smiling mysteriously. "Nothing at all." Then I floated up the stairs.

"There's something wrong with Jo," I heard him say to Mother in the kitchen.

I decided I'd better try to act totally normal all evening. I knew what awful teases my brothers were if they found the slightest thing to tease about, and this would be just the sort of thing they looked for.

Upstairs in my room I caught a glimpse of myself in my mirror and came down to earth again very rapidly. No wonder Rick hadn't flipped at the sight of me. I was hardly Miss Seductive of the Year. My hair was matted to my head from perspiration, and my T-shirt hung, three sizes too large, disguising any figure I might have had.

I faced facts. I wasn't in Angie's class by a long way. If I wanted to get a boyfriend like everyone else, I was going to have to learn some of their rules. Angie and company had been practicing for years, and I was going to have to take a crash course on being a girl overnight.

I tore the rubber band from my hair and attacked it with a brush, blinking back the tears as it tore through the tangles. When it was nicely brushed, it framed my face and didn't look bad at all. I grabbed the comb and used it to hold my hair back a little from my face. The result was surprising. With my hair falling around it, my face looked slimmer and more interesting.

I decided to get on my bike and go and buy some barrettes before dinner. And maybe I'd get some eye shadow, too, I thought—pale green, or blue-green to highlight my large, greenish-brown eyes. Then I should really get some mascara, although I already had nice long, dark lashes.

By way of experiment I sneaked into my mother's room and feeling like a naughty two-year-old, I raided her makeup tray. I hadn't done that since I was a preschooler and Martin and I had made each other up like clowns. Mother was so mad because we squashed her favorite lipstick that I had never dared to touch her makeup again. My mother is normally such a quiet, placid person that when she does get mad it is terrifying. And so now, all these years later, I couldn't help glancing behind me as I put on the eye shadow. I was so pleased with the result that I tried a trace of lipstick.

Then I hurried to get to the store and be back for supper. I was running down the stairs, two at a time as usual, when I passed Martin again.

"Woweee! Look at you!" he yelled. "Mom—I told you Jo had flipped. Come and look at her now, quick!"

But I pushed him out of the way and rushed out to my bike.

By the time I got back, hot and tired after climbing the same hill twice in one day, I had spent every cent of my allowance—the allowance I had been saving to have my racket restrung. I had bought not only the makeup but a T-shirt that caught my eye in a store window. It was pale blue and edged with blue satin ribbon. When I tried it on, I really wanted some jeans to go with it, but the white jeans the saleswoman brought me to try on were twenty-eight dollars—not the sort of thing that could come out of my allowance. They would have to be coaxed out of a loving father at the right moment. After all, it wasn't often that I played up the advantages of being the only daughter.

This time I slunk in quietly, looking around me like a spy before I dashed up to my room. Then I carefully scrubbed off all the makeup, tied my hair back, and hid the T-shirt before I showed up at the dinner table, looking, I hoped, just like my usual self.

"I don't notice anything different," Peter said as soon as I walked in. "She looks as grubby as usual to me."

"But I told you, she was wearing makeup, and she had this silly grin on her face," Martin said, eyeing me suspiciously.

"Don't you guys know it's rude to discuss someone in front of them?" I said haughtily.

They ignored me and went right on.

"Yeah, maybe you're right," Peter said, looking at me as if I were an exhibit in a museum. "There is something different about her. You don't suppose she's found out she's a girl at last, do you?"

"Mother, will you make them stop?" I called to my mother, who was bringing the last dish in from the kitchen.

"Yes, you two bullies, leave the poor girl alone," my mother said, but she was smiling.

"But, Mom, we have to solve this mystery," Martin said. "You didn't see her this afternoon, but I did. And she did not look like her usual self."

"I know," Peter said brightly. "You don't suppose she's in love, do you?"

I tried desperately to stop myself from

blushing, but the color flooded to my cheeks anyway. The boys looked gleeful.

"Ha, ha! That's what it is! Mom, we've found out what's wrong with Joanna—she's in love!" Martin shouted.

"Shut up, Martin. I hate you," I yelled and swung a punch in his direction.

"Watch it, Martin. Women in love are known to be very touchy," Peter said, then ducked as I threw a spoon in his direction.

"Who *is* the lucky guy?" he went on.

"Will you both leave me alone—I don't want to talk about it."

"Oh, you see, he's so ugly that she doesn't want anyone to know about him—"

"Or else he's a moron—"

"Come on, Jo. Don't leave us in suspense."

"I said I don't want to talk about it. Now cut it out, will you? I don't bug you about your girlfriends."

"Don't worry," Martin said. "If she won't tell, I can soon find out. I'll just send out my spies at school, have her followed all day—"

"Yeah—catch them kissing in the chemistry lab," Peter said.

"I think you're both obnoxious," I yelled and ran out of the room.

Later that evening, I thought things over. It was definitely time to shed the tomboy image, but it was going to be tough. I had a lot to learn. If becoming a girl overnight meant getting this kind of abuse, I wasn't sure it was worth it. However, at least I must have done something right to have gotten a reaction from my brothers. Maybe I would become a regular girl after all.

Chapter Six

The next day I left very late to go to school. I waited in my room until I heard Peter's car leave for college and Martin's bike scrunch across the gravel. Then I tiptoed downstairs, only to meet my father coming up them.

"My, but don't you look nice," he said, nodding his head in approval. "Is it a special day or something?"

"Yes. It's—pictures for the yearbook," I lied and hurried past him before the blush could appear.

The effect at school was instant, too, and I was amazed at the compliments. At lunch Dee Dee tried to be nonchalant when she exclaimed, "Jo, I love your hair like that!" I was surprised at how much her approval mattered to me.

"I think de Mayo's just found out she's a

girl," said Artie. Vowing to be ladylike in my behavior from now on, I did not punch him.

Everyone seemed impressed with me. Everyone, of course, except Rick. After school I changed my jeans for my white tennis skirt and kept on the soft blue T-shirt, brushed my hair (itself a minor miracle as I usually touched it only once a day) and tied it back with a blue ribbon, and went down to the tennis courts.

Rick was already there, with two other boys. The other two looked up approvingly, but Rick still scowled.

"I hear you're going to be the fourth boy on our team," said a tall, dark-haired boy. He gave me a big smile that made me feel good. "Hi, I'm Tony Johnstone," he said. "I know your brother." He looked familiar, and I remembered he had come to our house with Martin once.

I smiled back at him. "Yes, I remember you came to our house once."

"And I met you?" he asked. "You weren't that tough little kid that yelled something nasty, were you? Boy, how you've grown up!"

The other guy looked shyly in my direction. "Hi, I'm Bill," he said, peering at me from behind large, horn-rimmed glasses.

"Don't expect him to say anything else," Tony said. "He's the strong, silent type. He only allows himself two words a week, and he's just used those up."

Bill grinned but said nothing more. Tony was obviously the social one. "Coach Parker tells us you've got a fantastic serve," he said. "Oh, by the way, have you already met Rick?"

"Yes," I said, trying to sound cool and disinterested. "We've already met."

For a moment Rick's eyes met mine. "At least you look like a girl today," he said. "But that's not going to get you special treatment around here. If you want to be on the boys' team, you're going to have to work as hard as any of the guys."

"Don't worry, I intend to," I said. "I've been playing at least two hours of tennis every day for the last six years, so I should be used to it by now."

"Yeah, but this is play against boys, not pat ball," said Rick, glaring at me defiantly.

I felt my temper boiling up. "I thought you said you were going to quit the team if I joined," I said scornfully. "So how come you're still here?"

Of course, I regretted saying it immediately. After all, you hardly get a boy to start liking you by saying spiteful things to him. But my trouble was that sometimes my tongue got the better of me and said things before I could stop it.

Rick's eyes flashed at this challenge. "I'm only here because I thought it over, and I decided that if our team has to stoop to taking girls, we must be in pretty bad shape. We're going to need all the help we can get. But don't think it means I agree to having you on our team. Girls belong on a girls' team. If you play on this one, you'll just be keeping some boy from having a chance to play tennis!"

"Oh, knock it off, Rick," Tony said. "You know as well as I do that we need another good player this year. Bill and I are fine for the doubles, but there just isn't another singles player. All the jocks went out for baseball or swimming this year."

"All right, everyone, let's get started. Don't hang around talking," Coach Parker called as he came out of the gym. "Start warming up. Tony, you play with Joanna down at the other end."

As I walked beside Tony I couldn't help asking, "Just what does Rick have against me?"

He smiled. "Oh, nothing personally." (That was, at least, reassuring.) "It's against girls in general." (That was not.) "He comes from a sort of old-fashioned family where the father gives the orders and expects his mother to obey. He's got three sisters who he always has to look out for and entertain—his old man is always on to Rick about how boys should take care of girls. He's not used to competing against girls, and I think he feels a little threatened by you. But he'll come around in the end. Don't worry. And don't let him bug you. Anyway, Bill and I are happy about having you on the team, and if Coach Parker says you're good, then that's enough for me. He's a good coach, and he doesn't hand out praise too often."

"Get moving, you two. If you want to stand around gossiping, you can do it in your own time, not mine!" Coach Parker bawled.

"He's also a slave driver," said Tony, grinning as he hit the first ball.

In spite of everyone's reassurances that Rick would come around to wanting me on the team, as the days went by he still showed no sign of softening. In fact, he was more hostile than ever. But under the hostility I knew that, besides being a pretty good tennis player, he was a terrific person. I could tell that he was sensitive and thoughtful by the way he treated the guys on the team. He just had this blind spot about athletic girls.

But by the end of the week, his constant teasing and sarcastic remarks started getting to me. My concentration began to suffer, and I started missing some easy shots.

"Look at that," Rick jeered. "The Iron Maiden is not absolutely perfect. Miss Wonderful just missed my forehand lob."

"Why don't you give her a break?" Tony said angrily. "You've been bugging her all week. She's as good a player as you are."

"That may be true, but we'll still be the laughingstock of the state if we have a girl on a boys' team."

"Not if we win, we won't!" Tony said.

"But to get beaten by a girl!" Rick said with disgust.

"I wouldn't mind," said Bill thoughtfully. He never said much and always thought for a long while before he spoke, but what he said always made good sense. "If a girl player is better than me, then she's better. No big deal."

"I think you're both nuts," Rick snapped.

"And I think you're afraid she's going to take the number-one slot away from you."

"That'll be the day." Rick laughed, but I saw in his face that Tony had hit home. It was obvious to everyone but Rick that that was part of his problem. He saw me as a threat— not just to his masculine pride but for the number-one position.

I even began to think that if that was all it took to make him happy and to make him like me, then he could have his number-one slot. Maybe I could be content to be number two, even if I knew very well that I could be number one.

The fact that I now knew where I stood as a tennis player did wonders for my morale. And the fact that I was dressing to please Rick and kept getting compliments also didn't hurt my self-esteem. I found that I was no longer slinking around school scowling at people and acting like a social outcast. I found that I had had a big chip on my shoulder before and that I had thought people were teasing me when they were only being friendly.

So, in spite of the fact that I was having one big, long fight with Rick, I still looked forward to going to school more each morning. Even when I bumped into someone from the girls' tennis team, I didn't feel the panic and desire to run I would have felt before.

And best of all, there was tennis practice. I had always loved playing, even those long hours by myself against the training wall. But now, as I got better, the thrill of returning a hard smash or going up for a high lob was even greater.

One day I was standing at the notice board,

reading the boys' team schedule, and I looked up to see Jackie looking at the girls' team information on the next board.

"Well, hi," she drawled, then went back to studying her girls' team match schedule. "I see you didn't make the team after all," she said in a pitying voice. "That's tough luck. I thought you were pretty good. You know you played very well that day, and I was kind of afraid for a while that you might have edged me out of my place." She smiled at me then, and I realized she was feeling sorry for me. After all, I had seen the same look from Angie many times: "Poor Joanna, always a loser."

But I was learning to play more than one game. I was learning that instead of lashing out with fake bragging, I could achieve more by holding my temper. In fact, I was getting pretty good at the people game. I smiled now. "It's okay," I said. "The boys' coach thought that I was good enough, so now I'm on the boys' team."

I hoped it had come out with the right balance of modesty and confidence. I didn't want to sound like I was bragging, but I wasn't about to let her put me down, either. It obviously had the right effect because Jackie looked surprised and then managed an almost sincere, "Oh . . . congratulations."

"Thanks," I said, and let the subject drop.

As I walked off, I said to myself, "Watch out, Oakview High. The new, improved Joanna de Mayo is definitely growing up."

Chapter Seven

Besides being fun, playing with the tennis team was also hard work. I used to think I worked myself hard when I practiced in the mornings, but my workout was nothing compared to this. Coach Parker was, as Tony predicted, a slave driver. He told us he wanted us to win the State High School Cup at the end of the season, and if we worked hard enough, there was no reason why we shouldn't. Every practice session started with warm-ups and stretches to make our muscles supple and strong, sprints on the track for bursts of speed, and miles of jogging to build up endurance. On the court there were long drills with the ball machine. The ball machine is a fiendish torture instrument that spews out balls mechanically, fast or slow, high or low, according to how the coach sets it. The trouble is that with a ball machine you can never beat it, and you can never rest between shots. Coach Parker would make me stand at the net while balls came flying at me, then he would yell at me to put one in the right-hand corner, the next in the left.

But even though the workouts were hard, I began to feel better about my tennis. It was as if suddenly something special was within my grasp. I knew I could be good. I thought maybe I could be *very* good one day, even as good as Greg if I worked hard. And work hard I did. I came home drenched in sweat every afternoon, with muscles so tired that passing the butter at dinner was an act beyond my strength.

"Poor old Jo," the family would tease as I struggled up the stairs to bed. "She's on her last legs." Then they would plan my funeral with Peter preaching a very solemn eulogy and Martin singing "Abide with Me" mixed with the latest rock 'n' roll tune. They would try to make me laugh, knowing that my stomach muscles hurt me so much that I wouldn't dare.

I put up with this new teasing because it kept their minds off questions about my new "love," whom Martin had still not uncovered at school. And however exhausted I was physically, my family knew how happy I was and were unanimous that I was a much better person to have around now that I had "found myself."

"Her temper is a lot better," I heard Martin telling Dad as they were washing the car together. "Do you know that she hasn't kicked me once since she started this tennis team?"

That's because I haven't had the energy to spare, I thought. Don't push your luck.

"She's looking pretty good, too," Dad said. "Taking a pride in her appearance. I'm glad to see that. Frankly, I was worried about her for a while."

As the workouts continued, I began to feel better. My muscles ached less, and I knew I was becoming stronger. And another good thing started to happen. Rick started to thaw a little.

When he saw me completing all the workouts—the exercises, the jogging, and the ball machine, working as hard as he did and never complaining, which he did sometimes, I could see that he was gradually coming to the conclusion that maybe I was OK after all. When he talked to me, which admittedly wasn't often and was usually about tennis (exciting things like, "There's a new can of balls on the bench that Coach wants us to use"), he no longer had a sneer in his voice. And if we were playing and I hit a good shot he actually said, "Good return," or "Nice lob."

Of course, when he did that I floated at least five feet off the tennis court, and since it's much harder to field balls from that height, my play went berserk for a while.

Then came one memorable day when I leaped for an impossible overhead, landed awkwardly, and fell over backward. Rick was my partner, and he rushed over looking concerned and said, "Are you okay?"

Unfortunately, I was. I toyed with the idea of acting helpless and in agony so he'd have to help me up. But instead I got up and brushed myself off as casually as possible.

"I'm fine, thank you," I said, wishing I weren't.

Secretly, I wanted to have sprained my ankle and to have been carried off the court in Rick's strong arms, then to sit in the locker room while Rick tenderly applied ice packs to a dramatically swelling ankle. In fact, I would have gone through a lot of pain and agony to have been carried off by Rick. But I wouldn't fake it. I may have stopped swaggering around, but I wasn't ready to go that far the other way.

I tried to be realistic as I lay in bed that

night and the warm tingling glow kept making my toes curl up. Over and over I relived that scene—seeing Rick's concerned face and hearing, "Are you OK?" as he came toward me.

"Don't read things into that, Joanna," I warned myself sternly. "Don't think that he suddenly cares about you. It's only that he knows you're a good tennis player, and he doesn't want you to be out of the opening game next week."

But at its very worst his action proved that I was getting somewhere with him. At least he didn't ignore me or step over me or make a sarcastic remark about girls not being able to stand on their own feet. Yes, progress was definitely being made!

The next morning he actually stopped me in the hall and said, "Are you still in one piece after that fall yesterday?"

"I'm fine, thanks. Only a couple of bruises in places that I can't show you."

He laughed. "Good for you. See you after school." Then he waved and walked on. I felt as if somebody had just awarded me the Nobel Prize.

I'm glad that I had one whole day of ecstasy, for right after school the blow struck.

"Come over here, and hurry, you guys," Coach Parker called as we were on our way out to the court. "I want to talk to you about our first meet on Saturday. We're playing Huntington Park, and you know they're tough. Their number-one player is state ranked, and he's had a lot of tournament experience. I want the opening match against him to be our strongest possible. If we can beat him, then we have the rest of them psychologically, because they are counting on him for their points." He looked from Rick to me and back to Rick again. "So the question is, who do we put against him?"

Four people stared at him, nobody wanting to be the first to speak up.

"What I'd like to do," Coach Parker said, "is have Rick and Joanna out here at lunchtime tomorrow to play a three-set match. Whoever wins that, I'll put in our number-one position. That seems to be the fairest way to do it."

I took a hurried look at Rick's face. He was staring down at the concrete, frowning. His lips were in that tight line again. He really wanted to be number one. It flashed through my mind that if I won the game, I'd lose him forever.

All the way home, I thought about it. So you just don't win. You let him win and live happily ever after as number two. Fine. But . . . there were several buts. What if he was more nervous than I was, and I won anyway? What if Coach Parker saw me missing shots on purpose? He was no fool, and he would know right away if I was not playing my hardest. What if Rick guessed that I was letting him win? That would do more to hurt his pride than my really beating him fair and square. And, last, a nagging doubt that I tried to shut out: could I live with myself and my ambitions if I knew that I had lost on purpose?

I tried out all sorts of solutions. I would be sick, and then Rick would have to be number one. No. Then Coach Parker would only make us play the next day or the day after that, and I couldn't stay out of school indefinitely. Whatever I tried, it all came back to this: if I stayed on the team, Rick and I would have to play each other in the end. And if we did play, I didn't know if I could let myself lose.

Then I finally came up with a solution. I would tell Coach Parker that these workouts were too much for me and they were affecting my health and my grades. Therefore, I had made up my mind to go back to the girls' team. I felt a terrible pang of pain as soon as I thought of that—no more Coach Parker as my coach, no more Tony and Bill to joke around with, and no more seeing Rick every day. But if it meant there was a chance with Rick, maybe it was worth it. Perhaps he would know as soon as he heard I was quitting that I was quitting for him, so that he wouldn't be shown up in front of the other boys. Then he would be grateful to me—perhaps even more than grateful. Maybe he would realize what a sacrifice I had made for him and how much I liked him!

I had my speech all planned out by the time we met with Coach Parker at lunch.

Coach listened without saying anything. I think I hoped he would forbid me to leave, would tell me how much I was needed on his team. But his face displayed no emotion whatsoever as I gave him my reasons. I looked across at Rick's face then. He was listening in disbelief, and then he grinned.

As soon as I had finished and before Coach Parker could say anything, Rick jumped in. "What did I tell you, Coach? I knew it was only a matter of time before the pace got too much for her."

That really made me see red. I reacted just the way I had to Scott McKinley's challenge in third grade. Rick might be the cutest boy in the world, and I might be turning down my one chance with him, but I didn't think of any of those things now. I didn't care who he was at that moment—Prince Charles or Robert Redford—he was not going to get away with a remark like that. Over my dead body was he going to get away with a remark like that!

"I take back everything I said," I snapped. "I'm perfectly willing to go on playing on the boys' team. Go get your racket and we'll see which of us is going to be number one!"

Then I stalked toward the court. I caught a glimpse of Coach Parker's grin out of the corner of my eye. He looked as if he were expecting something like this to happen. Well, he might think it was funny, but I certainly didn't. Of course, about halfway to the court I began to realize what I had done. I had now lost Rick forever. I almost turned around and went back, but my pride and stubbornness were a legend in my family, and they would not let me go back.

There was an eerie silence as we stood in two far corners of the court and took off our racket covers. Coach Parker walked across to the net and took his position as umpire. It was hot that noon, unusually hot for April, and the new leaves hung without stirring on the dusty trees. Even the birds seemed to have fallen asleep, and the drone of distant traffic was a noise that seemed to come from the heat itself. I felt as if I were in an unreal world, the sort of world that dreams are made of. My arms and legs felt strange and heavy, as if I were moving in slow motion. When we started to warm up, the only sound was the monotonous thwack of the ball hitting strings. Then when we finally started to play, the sound of Coach Parker's voice was added to this, calling out the points with studied indifference—"Forty-fifteen. Game, Joanna."

One thing I had been wrong about. Rick did not seem to be nervous, and if he was, it was not affecting his tennis. He stood there, tight-lipped, eyes crinkled against the sun, waiting, tense as a spring about to uncoil, to receive my service.

I wasn't nervous, either. This was the first really important match of my life, and I felt my family heritage coming out. I was my father, standing without any display of emotion on the sidelines while the opposing team was on his ten-yard line. I was Greg, two sets down to Bjorn Borg, strolling casually to change ends without taking a sip of Gatorade. I felt as if I weren't a person at all, but a robot programmed to hit the ball in the right way at the right time, to the right place.

For the first eight games, we both held our services. It was as if we were each testing the strength of the other. Then on the ninth game I felt an extra surge of energy. It was the high feeling of total concentration that I sometimes got after playing with Greg for a while. My first serve flashed down the center line. So did my second and third, and I won a love game. That was obviously the crack in his morale I needed, for Rick made several unforced errors in the next game, and I was able to take the set, six games to four.

But I was not confident (or stupid) enough to think I had him beaten. The second set he fought for every point, leaping right across court to return impossible volleys or running back to return deep lobs. His face was a brilliant red from the heat, and I expect mine was, too, but I wasn't conscious of feeling hot. I wasn't conscious of anything except the will to win.

The game went on and on. Every service seemed to go to deuce again and again. The robot was beginning to turn back into a human being. I began to notice the sweat trickling down between my shoulders and running into my eyes. My mouth felt parched, as if I had been lost for days in the desert.

This time nobody dropped a service. We were even. Six games each.

"Play a twelve-point tie breaker," Coach Parker said, "or this will go on all afternoon."

Dizzy with exhaustion, I staggered to my position.

"And you think you want to be a professional one day," I jeered at myself. "You're washed out after two sets. What if you had to play day after day, set after set? You couldn't hack it, just like Rick said."

I hadn't seen this possibility before—that he might really beat me. I had thought I was the superior player. I was, too, in the quality of my tennis, but in stamina? Were boys really more hardy than girls?

I realized that this afternoon Rick was playing his heart out. There was more in this at stake for him than for me. Then I thought of the whispers around school: "Everyone said she was the best player, but she wasn't as good as Rick after all. . . . She looks good in practice, but she cracks under pressure. . . ."

"I do not," I said and was embarrassed to hear myself say it out loud. I looked up in case Rick and Coach Parker had heard me. But Rick was waiting, still as a statue, for me to serve.

Suddenly I realized that if I lost this tie breaker, it would be one more whole set to get through. Not another set, I thought. Not in this heat. No way!

It was as if someone pressed a button and switched me back into high gear. I found the energy to serve, then to leap forward to take the return at the net. I stood poised for Rick's serves and sent them zinging back into impossible corners of the court. I quickly got the seven points I needed for victory.

When it was all over, the coach came up and shook both our hands. "Nice playing, both of you," he said. "Looks like I got me a winning team this year. You should both be proud of playing like that!"

It was true—I did feel proud and exhilarated, but at the same time I felt incredibly sad. I expected Rick to turn and walk away or to come out with some bitter, sarcastic statement. Instead, his eyes met mine.

"Congratulations," he said quietly. "Anyone who can win every point in a tie breaker deserves to be number one."

Chapter Eight

It was, in fact, a lot easier to beat the famous, state-ranked, number-one seed from Huntington Park than it was to beat Rick. When we arrived at Huntington Park early on Saturday morning and I walked out in my tennis dress onto the middle of the court, the boy's face broke into an amused grin.

"You're their number one?" he asked snidely. "Or is this some sort of joke?"

"No joke," I said. "I'm the number one."

"I didn't know Oakview was that desperate this year," he said.

"Be gentle with her, Smitty," one of his supporters yelled. The other kids laughed. I blushed slightly, but I tried to keep my cool and walked slowly to my end of the court.

Smitty was so sure that he could beat me without trying that he was careless. I played a defensive game, standing ready on the base line for one of his careless shots. By the time he realized he was losing and started to play desperately, I switched to an attacking game, and he had no chance of catching up.

Our few supporters went wild, and I felt elated. But I tried very hard not to let it show. I tried to make my face look as if I ate state-ranked players for breakfast every day. I walked up to the net and shook his hand.

"Good game," I said politely, although it hadn't been for him.

The rest of the matches that day were a disaster for Huntington Park. They were psychologically beaten the moment I thrashed their star, and Rick and the boys cleaned up on them in straight sets.

I think it was then that the boys on my team began to see, if they had not seen before, the wisdom of having a girl on their team. After all, no boy expects to have to play hard to beat a girl, and my play was so consistent that once I got ahead they couldn't catch up with me.

The best thing about the whole day was Rick. He came and sat beside me in the school bus going home—without being asked to, and with extra seats available!

"Maybe you should teach me how to do that

passing shot you used today," he said. "If I try that, it goes cross-court, not straight down the line like yours did."

"It's not hard," I said. "It's a question of which foot your weight is on."

"Where did you learn all those things? Have you had professional coaching?"

"Are you kidding? My father is a college football coach, and you know they don't get paid that kind of money. None of us kids ever had professional coaching. My brother taught me everything I know."

"Well, lucky you to have a brother like that," Rick said. "I've only got sisters, and I guess I haven't learned much from them."

It's funny how you piece people together bit by bit like a jigsaw puzzle. I learned something else about Rick then, not from what he said, but from what he didn't say and from his sigh. He didn't really like his sisters very much and probably only saw them as helpless things he had to look out for and take care of. He'd obviously had enough of being used by girls.

We talked all the way home, mainly about tennis, but by the time we were back at school we had relaxed with each other. Rick was beginning to look upon me as another human being. I was dizzy with success. From here it was only a step to being looked upon as a special human being!

The school bus swung into the yard.

"See ya Monday!" we called to each other as we climbed down.

I had just stepped off the bus and was walking away, when a beautiful girl with long blonde hair brushed past me.

"I thought you were never coming, Rick," she called. "Come on, the others are waiting in the car."

I didn't turn around to watch him greet her. Instead, I hurried out of the parking lot, feeling as if someone had just punched me in the stomach. Why did perfect days always have to end so badly? What competition was I for a girl who looked like that?

I remembered Rick grinning to the coach about his "heavy date." I might be able to beat him on the court, but off court I was still a loser!

But even a big letdown like seeing Rick's girlfriend could not entirely take away the pleasure of my win. I told my family about it as soon as I got in the door, and they said nice things like, "All right, Jo," and "Well, you can't be as bad as we thought you were," but they didn't make any big thing of it. After all, they were pretty used to winning de Mayos by this time.

* * *

I didn't think it was anything extraordinary either until I arrived at school on Monday morning. During the first period I got a summons to go to the principal's office.

"What've you been up to, de Mayo?" one of the boys asked, laughing.

"Yeah, you should stop smoking in the bathrooms," another teased.

As I left the room I heard the murmur of speculation about what crime such a blameless person as I could have committed. I began to get worried myself. I knew, when I examined it logically, that I hadn't done anything wrong, but calls to the principal's office were usually reserved for the worst degree of school criminals. So it was with a slightly trembling hand that I knocked on his door.

Mr. Dixon beamed when he saw me.

"Ah, Joanna, there you are. Come right in."

I was surprised—not by the warmth of the welcome, but that he even knew me from Adam.

"Miss Soames, this is Joanna," he said, and I noticed for the first time that an elegant-looking woman was sitting in the corner of his office. She got up and extended a beautifully manicured hand in my direction.

"So glad to meet you," she said warmly.

To say I was bewildered was an understatement. I hadn't a clue what was going on. I looked hopefully at Mr. Dixon for an explanation. He smiled at me. "Joanna, this is Miss Soames from the *Huntington Reporter*," he said. "She's here to do a story on you."

"On *me*?" I asked.

He smiled again. "Yes. It seems that the story of your tennis playing is spreading far and wide. Anyway, why don't I step out of my office for a while, and then you can interview in peace."

With that he left. I looked uneasily at the woman. As soon as the door closed she became all action, getting out her little notebook and pencil and turning toward me with, "What was your reason for going out for the boys' team? Did you want to prove that girls can do anything boys can do, or did you feel that the girls' program was inadequately funded to provide equal opportunity?"

I realized instantly what answers she was looking for and what direction she wanted her story to take.

I had never thought much about women's liberation. When I didn't make the football team, I had felt that life was unfair, but I accepted it the same way I accepted that I had to go to bed before my older brothers and eat my spinach before I got my dessert. I never really thought that competing against boys was proving anything other than the fact that I was just as good as some boys. I certainly didn't see myself as striking a blow for all women. But that was how Miss Soames saw it, apparently.

I thought very carefully before I answered now. Luckily my father had often been interviewed and quoted in papers, and he had often been very mad at the way they twisted his words. So I knew I mustn't answer without thinking, or I would come out sounding like something I was not.

"I didn't want to try out for the boys' team at all," I said.

"Oh?" She looked puzzled. "Why was that?"

"I would have been happy on the girls' team. I just love to play tennis."

"Oh." She sounded a little disappointed.

"But the boys' coach asked me to join his team because they needed another strong singles player."

"And were you flattered when they asked you?"

"I guess so."

"Why? Because you think boys are better tennis players than girls?"

"Of course not."

"So did you feel you were making a point

about women athletes by joining the team?"

"No. I just wanted to play some good tennis."

"Do you think that the girls' program is inferior?"

I was going to tell her about the cracks on the girls' courts with the grass growing in them and the coach who wasn't very qualified, but decided that that would start something I wasn't ready to get into. So instead I said, "I just think there's more competition on the boys' team right now."

"Well, you can obviously hit as hard as any boy. You beat Danny Smitt, who is highly ranked in this state. How come you can play such powerful tennis?"

"My brother taught me to play when I was very small, and he has been coaching me ever since. He hits very hard, and I learned that if I didn't hit hard back I usually got massacred."

"This would be your brother Greg—the professional?"

"That's right."

"Did you take up tennis to try to compete with him?"

"Actually I took it up because he came up to me one day when I was about seven, stuck a racket in my hand and said, 'Come on, kid. Today is the day you are going to learn tennis.' And pretty soon I started to love playing."

Miss Soames smiled, but I could see I had disappointed her. She had planned in her mind this wonderful article on a feminist tennis player striking a blow for the freedom of girls' sports everywhere, and I had now dashed her hopes. I had told her I had only taken up the sport because my brother made me and only joined the boys' team because my coach made me. And now I simply wanted to play tennis.

She gave up on that point. She did ask me a few more questions about my ambitions and my relationships to the boys on the team, and I answered vaguely to both, not wishing to give anything away about matters that were important to me. Then she had a photographer take a picture of me standing by the tennis net and clutching my racket.

I worried a lot about the article and whether it would twist my words to echo what Miss Soames wanted to hear. But when it came out, it was pretty wishy-washy and didn't mention my opinions at all. Just things about Oakview High having high hopes for its new young tennis star. There was a picture of me beside the article, and it looked pretty good, which was unusual, since I don't usually photograph well. Most pictures of me show me scowling or screwing my eyes up against the light, but this one looked like an attractive, confident tennis player.

My family was thrilled. Dad drove straight down to the nearest newsstand and bought up all the copies, and Mom cut out the article to send to Greg.

The photo worked wonders for me among the kids at school. Lots of upperclassmen, who had just ignored a sophomore like me, now stopped me on my way to class and said, "Hey, you must be Joanna de Mayo. I saw your picture in the paper. I didn't realize we had a celebrity at school." Dee Dee was genuinely happy for me, and even Angie seemed impressed.

The boys on the tennis team teased me all afternoon, bowing low whenever I came near them and asking for my autograph. But it was the friendly teasing of brothers, and it told me that I was accepted as one of them.

I got a letter from Greg at the end of the week. It said, "I see I'm going to have some competition soon. I'll be playing in Boston on the tenth and thought your team might like to come and watch the *good* de Mayo in action. Show this form at the door for reserved courtside seats."

Coach Parker and the boys were thrilled at the idea of free seats for the game. The coach was happy because we could watch strokes done correctly and learn some doubles tactics. The boys were happy because we got to miss afternoon workout.

Right after school we all set off in the coach's beat-up old station wagon, all chattering and giggling like little kids on a cub scout outing. "Who'd McEnroe draw in the first round?" "I hope we'll see Vilas." "I'd rather see Gerulaitis." "I think I might go out on that court and show those guys how!" "You? Don't make me laugh." I didn't mention my brother at all. Although the boys knew about him, I didn't want them to think I was showing off about having a pro in the family.

The auditorium was huge, and from the entrance halfway up, the court looked like a small square of light in a sea of darkness. The usher led us down and down, right to the very front row. We were so close to the court that we could almost reach out and touch the players. Our seats were separated from the others in a little loge, and we felt very special when the TV camera panned over us a couple of times before the game started.

"I bet they're trying to figure out if we're someone famous," Tony said.

"I bet they're saying, 'What's that gorgeous

girl doing with those scruffy boys in the front row?'" I said.

"Nonsense!" Tony laughed. "They're saying, 'Who are those handsome boys? They must be famous tennis stars from another country, and that girl with them is there to wash out their tennis clothes!'"

I didn't dare hit him in case the TV cameras were on me, but I murmured, "You just wait."

"By the way," Rick said suddenly, "how come we got these fantastic seats?"

"Joanna got them for us, dope. Didn't you know that?" Bill said.

"Nobody told me." Rick sounded hurt. "Someone just said we had free seats for a tennis match."

"Well, now that you know, you'd better thank Joanna nicely," Tony said.

"Thank you nicely," Rick said and touched my hand. I felt as if I had been hit with an electric shock. How come he still had the power to do things like this to me? Tony often touched me, put an arm around me, or grabbed my hand, and I felt nothing. But when I was within two yards of Rick, I was affected by his magnetic field!

To show that I was cool, calm, and positively not trembling, I opened my program.

My brother was in the first match. It was right there in big letters.

Rick leaned across to me, sending shock waves racing in my direction again. "Is that de Mayo in the program any relation of yours?"

"That's her brother, dope," Tony said in surprise. "Have you been asleep for the past few weeks?"

"That's really your brother?" Rick asked, shocked.

I nodded. "How else do you think we got tickets for something like this?"

He shook his head. "I really had no idea. I must not have been paying attention or something."

I knew exactly what had happened, but I was not going to tell him. At the time the others had found out about me, Rick was still sulking and stomping off. He had obviously shut out of his mind any talk about me. I had assumed everyone knew about my brother. After all, I had told him that my brother had coached me.

Then there was clapping, and four young men walked out, each carrying a bunch of rackets, chatting and laughing casually as if there weren't TV cameras all around and thousands of people staring at them. It was hard for me to believe that one of them was actually my brother, who had jumped down our stairs with a Tarzan yell and who once walked out of the house wearing my mother's only hat. He had let his hair grow long so that it hung over his collar. I grinned to myself. Dad would never have let his hair get that long at home.

The players reached their chairs beside the court and placed their rackets on them, each selecting one to play with. Greg was removing his warm-up jacket when he saw me, and with thousands of people watching, he walked right across the court to say hi!

"How you doing, kid?" he asked. "If I get too tired out there, I'm going to call on you to take over for me, so make sure you watch for my signal!"

"You just make sure you win," I said.

"With this whole band of supporters rooting for me, I couldn't lose," he said, winking. Then he turned and strolled back again.

When I realized that the TV cameras had been pointed at us, I nearly died of embarrassment. It was nice embarrassment, though.

Rick looked at me in awe. "That really was your brother, eh?"

"No, I always pick up strange tennis stars

when I go out," I said, my morale having been boosted by Greg actually noticing me and admitting he knew me in public. "Didn't you believe me before?"

"Sure I did," he said, but he didn't sound convinced.

I watched Greg like a hawk. He still played tennis like my brother, only he was more consistent now, more aggressive, and his serve was more accurate. But still recognizably my brother. Which made me think: if I were out there on that court I could return some of those balls. That made me feel hopeful about a future I hadn't wanted to reveal to the newspaper woman. Those players weren't totally out of my reach. I could be there one day.

Greg and his partner played well, but they were no match for the number-one seeds. It went to three sets, and they fought all the way, but in the end McEnroe and Ramirez out-classed them. But it had been a good match, and the crowd applauded warmly at the end. I positively glowed as my brother waved to me as he sauntered off.

After that there were two singles matches, and we saw both Vilas and Gerulaitis, which made Bill happy. We went home tired and happy, full of hot dogs and popcorn, and very silly. We sang little kid songs like "Bingo" and "She'll Be Coming Round the Mountain" all the way home in the car. It had been a good night.

Chapter Nine

Having a famous brother achieved something I might never have achieved alone. It made Rick Hendricks interested in me. When he offered to walk me home from school, I was not stupid enough to believe that it was for myself. I had mentioned at practice that day that Greg was staying with us for a few days, and Rick had said then that he would like to meet him. Still, I was also not stupid enough to turn down a chance to be walked home by Rick, whatever his motives were.

We talked very politely all the way home, and it was not until we reached our front gate that Rick said, "I don't suppose your brother will be in right now, will he?"

"Which brother?" I asked innocently. It was mean, I know, but I was enjoying myself.

"The tennis player."

"Oh, Greg? Yes, he'll be around, I'm sure.

When he comes home, all he does is eat and sleep."

Brief pause. I had a hard time stopping myself from laughing when I said, "Well, I guess I must be going in. Thank you for walking home with me."

"Yeah, sure," Rick answered and looked so disappointed that my hard heart melted. There was no way I could pay him back for all the teasing I had had to put up with, and what's more, I didn't want to pay him back or make him suffer.

"Don't you want to come in and meet him?" I asked.

His face lit up. "If you're sure that's all right."

"Of course it's all right. Come on in."

He grinned at me as I opened the gate. I walked ahead of him along the path and up the front steps.

This was the moment I had dreamed of for weeks. Of walking into our family room, having five pairs of eyes look up and greet me, and then being able to announce, "Mom, I'd like you to meet Rick."

That was exactly what happened today, but the triumph wasn't there. I wasn't able to slip my hand into his and say, "I'd like you to meet *my* Rick." Just, "I'd like you to meet

Rick—a boy on my tennis team. He wanted to stop by and meet Greg."

But the family looked up with interest anyway, and I saw Rick blush. He blushes, too, I thought, amazed by the many things we had in common!

"You don't want to meet Greg," said Martin, turning around from the ball game on TV. "He's the crazy member of the family."

"No more crazy than you are!" Greg muttered in mid-sandwich. As I had predicted, he was either eating or sleeping at home.

Peter was doing homework. He looked up with a serious expression. "Well, maybe Rick should realize right now that we are all crazy here! We live in straitjackets most of the time." Then he gave a really crazy laugh.

"And we sleep in padded cells," Martin added.

"Joanna, too, of course," said Peter. "So I wouldn't get too near her!"

Rick was looking from one to the other in amazement. My family is not only zany but very noisy if you aren't used to them.

When Peter made the remark about not getting too near me, I felt myself blush, and I saw Peter, who never misses anything, make a mental note for future teasing.

"Now, come on, you guys," my mother called

loudly enough to be heard over them all, "poor Rick is obviously not used to this kind of nonsense. He'll think you're all really crazy."

"But we are, dear Mother, and we inherited it from your side of the family," said Martin sweetly.

I began to wish I hadn't let Rick come home with me. Now that he knew about my weird family, he would never want to know me better. Perhaps he even believed that about the insanity—after all, looking at my brothers, it was easy to believe.

I turned and stole a quick glance in his direction. He was laughing. He was actually enjoying it!

My mother came over to him. "Don't mind them, Rick," she said. "They mean well. They're naturally very protective about Jo. They want to see what sort of person you are before they let her go out with you."

Mother! I let out a silent scream, sending panicky thought waves racing in her direction, pleading mentally, "Will you shut up! He doesn't want to take me out. He only came here to meet Greg!"

But out loud I said, "Rick came to get a chance to talk to Greg."

My mother, smiling a knowing smile, didn't believe me. But Greg, putting down his plate and rising from the sofa, where he had been curled like a cat, took the situation in hand beautifully. "You want to talk about tennis, Rick?" he asked. "How about we grab some rackets and go down to the court for a while? I didn't work out yet today."

Rick looked pleased, and I flashed Greg a grateful smile.

"You stay here, Jo," Greg said. "You're good enough already."

Then he led Rick out. As the door closed behind them, I exploded. "Mother, how could you do a thing like that to me?"

"Do what, dear?"

"Why, give him a lecture as if he was my boyfriend. Do you have any idea how that sounded: 'All the boys are very protective of Joanna. They want to see what sort of person you are.' I nearly died of embarrassment. It sounded as if he'd come to ask for my hand in marriage, not to meet Greg. He barely considers me a friend, to say nothing of a *girl-friend*."

"No, but you'd like him to."

"How did you know that?"

"It's written all over your face, darling. The moment you stepped into the room with him, your face said quite clearly, 'Here's someone I think is very special.'"

"Oh, no! Do you think he sees that, too? I don't want to scare him off. He's only just got over hating me."

"Hating you? Whatever for?"

"Because I took his place on the tennis team."

"Well, that sounds like a pretty good reason to me. But he's forgiven you now, hasn't he?"

"Yes."

"And he walked you home today. . . ."

"Only to meet Greg."

"Maybe the Greg bit was only an excuse because he's shy."

"I wish," I said sadly. "But all he wants to do is learn to serve like Greg. He still thinks I'm an overgrown tomboy."

My mother smiled again. "You wait and see," she said.

She sounded as if she had a dreadful plan up her sleeve. And she *did.* When Greg and Rick came back in the house, the first thing she did was invite Rick to stay for dinner, "so that he can have a chance to chat with Greg a little longer."

I herded Martin and Peter into the kitchen and begged them to behave themselves. "No fooling around, please, guys," I begged. "I don't ask you to do very much for me, but please behave like normal people at dinner tonight."

"Ah," said Peter, frowning at me, "but I have yet to discover whether he can keep you in the manner of craziness to which you are accustomed."

"Peter, he's not my boyfriend."

"That's what they always say. I read the *National Enquirer.* They always say, 'We're just good friends.'"

In spite of all my dreadful forebodings, Rick accepted our dinner invitation, and my brothers behaved reasonably well—for them. My father arrived home, chatted with Rick about tennis and football, and then we all went to the table. We got through the pot roast with no mishaps, although I sat alert, on the edge of my chair, ready to butt in on any wisecracks that could be taken the wrong way.

Then came dessert, and Daddy beamed when he saw it. "We've had a fantastic crop of strawberries this year," he proudly told Rick. "As big as golf balls, most of them."

"You're getting better, Dad," Peter said. "Yesterday you said they were as big as basketballs."

"I did not," my father said. "Baseballs, maybe, but not basketballs."

Since there had been no teasing and no embarrassing questions, I had begun to relax a little, even to enjoy the thrill of having Rick sitting opposite me at my own dinner table. I picked up the biggest, juiciest strawberry, and a thought popped, uninvited, into my mind.

"What's the difference between an elephant and a strawberry?" I asked.

Groans from all around. "Not more elephant jokes. I thought you'd finally grown out of them."

"What is the difference?" my father asked dutifully, knowing from long experience that I would go on until I was able to complete my joke.

"Well, if you don't know that, I wouldn't send you to pick strawberries," I said smugly.

"I know that one a different way," Rick said. "The answer to mine is that elephants are gray and strawberries are red—and then it goes on. What did Adam say when he saw a herd of elephants coming over the hill?"

"I don't know, what did he say?" I was stunned—an elephant joke that I hadn't heard before. I wouldn't have believed that such a thing existed.

Rick smiled. "He said, 'Look, there's a herd of elephants coming over the hill.' But what did Eve say?"

I thought about this for a moment. After all, I had had nine years of serious study in elephant jokes. I couldn't let one get the better of me. Suddenly I got it. "I know," I said triumphantly. "She said, 'Look, there's a herd of strawberries coming over the hill,' because she was color-blind."

"That's right!" Rick said in amazement.

"Don't tell me we've come across another elephant joke freak." Martin sighed. "One was bad enough."

Rick looked at me. "Most of my friends think elephant jokes aren't very sophisticated. It's good to know there's still someone around who thinks they're funny."

"Joanna knows over two hundred," Peter said. "But please don't ask her to tell you all of them right now."

"Maybe we should write a book of elephant jokes together," Rick said.

"And our super-sophisticated friends will be jealous when we're rich and famous," I said. I couldn't believe Rick and I were actually having this conversation!

"Whose turn is it to wash up?" my father asked.

"It's Joanna's, and I'm supposed to dry," said Martin.

"Well, I think we can let her off tonight since she's got a guest," said my father.

"No way!" said Martin. "You never let us off for any excuse. I had to wash last night, and I was late for baseball practice."

"That's OK. I don't mind washing up," I

said. I turned to Rick. "Our dishwasher gave up the ghost a couple of weeks ago, and we're still waiting for a new part to be delivered."

"I'll come and help," Rick said.

Out of the corner of my eye I saw my mother put out a hand and stop Martin from following us into the kitchen.

"Your family sure is noisy," Rick said when we were alone together.

"I know. I'm sorry about them. Now you see what I have to put up with all the time."

"Oh, I wouldn't apologize for them. I think they're great. You're lucky to have such a neat bunch of brothers. In my house no one ever raises their voice. My father still has this thing about 'a man's castle,' and the rest of us tiptoe around him most of the time."

"Well, as you can see, everyone gets a say in this house." I laughed.

"Your brother really helped me with my serve," Rick said. "He's a good teacher. So you'd better watch out, my girl. Now I know all of your tricks. . . ."

While he talked I had been playing with the mound of soapsuds that frothed in the sink. Then, before I could stop myself, I took two big handfuls and plopped them onto Rick's cheeks. "Not quite, you don't," I said.

Quick as lightning he grabbed both my hands.

"Oh, no, you don't," he said. "Thought you could get away with that, didn't you?"

He backed me against the sink, and we were very close to each other.

"Aren't you going to squeal for help?" he said.

"I never squeal," I whispered.

Then he kissed me. The soapsuds between our faces crackled and popped and disappeared, and we didn't even notice.

When at last we drew apart, he said, "Yech, I taste soap."

"Me, too."

We looked at each other and laughed, in wonder at what had happened.

"Will you forgive me?" Rick asked quietly.

"What for?"

"For being so mean to you. For not wanting you on the team?"

"Of course I forgive you. I forgave you long ago. I understand how you felt."

"You do?"

"Yes, I do."

"You know, after I found out what a great player you were, I didn't think you could be an ordinary girl, too. I thought of you as some sort of tomboy who wanted to play with the boys."

"Do you still think of me as a tomboy?" I asked, my eyes challenging.

"No way," he said, then kissed me again.

"You know," he said finally, "why didn't we see what a lot we had in common before? We like the same things, we are good at the same things, we act the same—"

"We have the same bad temper—"

"Exactly! We must have been made for each other from the start."

I didn't tell him that I had known that since day number one. But there was something I had to straighten out.

"Rick, what about your girlfriend?"

"My what?"

"Your girlfriend. I saw her the other day."

"Well, in that case you are good at seeing visions. My last girlfriend and I broke up before Christmas."

"But there was that girl who met you in the parking lot when we got off the bus. The one with the long blonde hair."

"You mean Serena? That was my sister. And she was bugging me, as usual."

"Your sister?" I squealed in delight. Of course, I had never turned around to see Rick's face; if I had I would have known and saved myself all that heartache.

"Yeah. My sisters are something else. I can't *go* anywhere without their turning up: 'Rick, you promised to drive us to the store'; 'Rick, you promised to fix my bike'; 'Rick, Mother says you have to stay home and cut the grass this afternoon.' I tell you, I wouldn't be at all surprised if one of them isn't spying in the kitchen window at this very moment."

"Well, I don't care," I said. "Let her spy if she wants to."

"And I don't care, either." He laughed. "Let's give her something worth watching, shall we?"

The third kiss was the best yet. I think practice was making perfect!

"Mom!" Martin called loudly. "I hope you have enough clean dishes for breakfast. I don't think much washing up is getting done in there."

Chapter Ten

If I had known that being in love was going to be as great as this, I would have started practicing for it like Angie had, way back in grade school. But on the other hand, the fact that it was all so new to me made it all the sweeter. My family teased me about floating down the stairs and passing the salt instead of the cornflakes at breakfast, and I didn't care. Most of the time I didn't even hear them.

When Rick and I came out to the tennis courts holding hands, Tony immediately burst out laughing. "When the coach said we had to get along together in this team, he didn't mean *that* well."

"Knock it off, Tony, you're only jealous," Rick said.

"Well, I hope you won't start wanting to hold my hand next," Tony said.

"Don't worry, old man." Rick laughed. "I'm

very particular about whose hand I hold, and frankly, you're not my type."

Bill, as usual, said nothing. He just sat there and grinned. Even though we were no longer holding hands by the time Coach Parker came out, he noticed right away.

"It's about time you two thickheads saw what was obvious to me from the start."

"And what was that, Coach?" Rick asked.

"Why, that you two are good for each other—same terrible temper, same stupid sense of humor—"

"Same fantastic tennis!" Rick added quickly.

"Well, I certainly hope so," the coach said fiercely. "I'm expecting great things from you two. Don't forget that the High School Cup is a doubles event, and I'm counting on you two to win it for the first time in the history of the school."

"You mean you didn't win it when Greg was on the team?" I asked delightedly.

"I said it was doubles," Coach Parker replied. "The trouble was that year I only had one Greg. The rest of the team was awfully weak. Even Greg couldn't cover the whole court all the time. They were beaten easily. But you two . . . you're going to make a great team, aren't you? Now don't just stand there loafing around. Get out there and hit some balls. And don't waste my time by standing there, grinning at each other like idiots!" But I saw he was smiling, and later, after the others had gone, he held me back and told me that he was glad Rick and I had worked out our problems. "After all," he said, "now you can devote all your emotional tension to your tennis."

The first few days of being in love were like waking up to Christmas every morning. I would open my eyes, and as I focused on the pattern of leaves dancing in the sunlight across my ceiling, I would wonder what was so special about today and why I felt so good. Then I would remember and heave a huge sigh of happiness. As I dressed I would gaze out of my window and wonder if the view had always been that perfect. Had there always been lilacs blooming, and had the early morning mist always draped itself across the distant hills, and were there always that many beautiful birds landing on our apple trees and singing their hearts out?

Then I would rush downstairs, grab a few bites of breakfast, and run all the way to meet Rick. Boring days at school became full and wonderful. Even something as small as an elephant joke he didn't know was a highlight of the day, a special secret to be shared between us. His sense of humor, as Coach Parker had mentioned, was as bad as mine, and we started playing some terrible tricks on each other. To have someone to laugh with was the most important thing of all. I felt like a foreigner, who, after years of living in a land where nobody speaks a word of her language, suddenly finds a fellow countryman at last.

One afternoon I took Rick up to the tree-house, and suddenly it was no longer a place of sad memories but as magical as the first day it had been built. Rick loved it.

"Wow. Look at the view from up here. You can spy on people coming all the way up the hill, and they would never see you."

"Which is exactly what I used to do when I was little. I used to have a trapeze on that branch, and sometimes I used to drop on people and scare the daylights out of them."

"That I can believe," he said. "In fact, I would believe anything at all about you." Then he rubbed his elbow. We had just been in a wrestling match, and I had thrown him, using a judo hold Peter had taught me.

"Yes," he went on, "I've decided that I'd better stay on the right side of you forever or get beaten to a pulp."

"Of course, I can be tamed," I said sweetly. "If you know the secret method."

"Like this?" Rick asked, drawing me to him and kissing me very gently.

"That method," I whispered, "works every time. . . ."

Then a second later he had turned from Rick the lover to Rick the joker. A couple of women were walking up the hill under our tree. Suddenly Rick let out a scream. "Help, help. No, stop it, you beast!" he cried in a high voice.

The women paused and looked alarmed. They were trying to find out where the voice was coming from.

"No, no. Don't you touch me, or I'll scream!" Rick went on.

"Rick!" I pleaded, and tried to put my hand over his mouth. We both fell to the floor, rolling over laughing. The tree shook alarmingly. The women looked up, then hurried off as fast as they could.

"Rick, you are terrible," I scolded. "Do you realize what you've just done? What will everyone think? Suppose they call the police or something?"

"I just thought I would teach you never to throw me again when we were wrestling," he said quietly.

It was certainly not a dull romance.

* * *

That weekend I went to meet his family. As soon as I stepped into his house, I could tell why he enjoyed being with my family so much. His house was a direct contrast to ours. Ours was always a jumble of friendly clutter. Nobody in my family was particularly tidy, and six not-so-tidy people together make one very untidy house. Rick's house, at first glance, looked like a furniture polish commercial. All the surfaces gleamed and shone without a speck of dust on them. The white glove test would have passed with flying colors here! There were lots of tiny tables and shelves, and on all of them were china ornaments—dogs and ballerinas and flowers. It was the sort of house where you don't dare move for fear of breaking something.

I stood and held my breath. Then Rick's mother came to meet us. "I'm so pleased to meet you, Joanna, dear," she said. "Rick's told us so much about you. Won't you sit down?"

The sofa, with its embroidered pillows, didn't look as if anyone ever sat on it, so I lowered myself carefully to the edge of a high-backed chair. Rick's mother sat on the edge of a wooden chair, and Rick moved across to stand beside me. We smiled politely at each other, then Rick started telling her about me and tennis and the cup we were training for. That gave me a good opportunity to study her. She was a tiny, pale woman, elegantly but not fashionably dressed in plain, dark colors. Her grayish hair was put up in a bun, which made her look older than she probably was. She looked as fragile as her own china. It was hard to imagine how someone as delicate as she looked could have produced such a large, healthy son as Rick.

I also noticed that he now moved quietly and carefully around the furniture, while away from home he took giant strides I could hardly keep up with.

The way his mother fussed about all the time was making me nervous. "More iced tea, Joanna? Are you sure? How about you, Rick? Not just half a glass more? Or a cookie? Why don't you have one of these cookies, Joanna? They're my own chocolate fudge. They're Rick's favorites, aren't they, Rick? Do try one, Joanna. Go on, don't be shy."

I hesitated because the cookies looked crumbly, and I had visions of something terrible happening to me if I dropped a crumb on the white carpet.

"Oh, do try one. I made them specially when Rick told me you were coming," she pleaded, so I had to take one. Then I thought I had solved the crumb problem by popping it into my mouth whole. Just as my lips closed around it, his mother asked, "Do you have plans for the summer yet, Joanna?"

Have you ever tried talking through a mouthful of dry cookie? I tried to mumble an answer, then choked on a crumb and spent the next few minutes sipping tea and trying to stop coughing. I don't think I was making a very good first impression.

When the afternoon was over, Rick seemed to be as relieved as I was. In fact, he came out smiling to himself and smiled all the way down the street.

"OK, what's so funny?" I demanded at last. "Did I say something wrong to offend the dignity of the Hendricks family?"

"No, no, you were perfect. She liked you, but when we were leaving, she said, 'I expected a girl tennis player to be a big beefy monster, but she looks almost normal.'"

"Thanks a lot," I said. "It's nice to know I'm *almost* normal."

"But think how boring you would be if you were only normal," Rick said, putting an arm around my shoulder. "And if it makes you feel any better, my family doesn't think I'm normal, either. So we go well together."

It was comforting to open my front door and be greeted by the crash of plates as Martin set the table, loud voices arguing over who should take out the garbage, my mother yelling for somebody to find the salt, and to trip over tennis shoes, books, T-shirts, and other things dropped by arriving de Mayos in the front hall. Home sweet home!

But meeting Rick's mother made me understand even better why he had reacted to me the way he had at first. If he'd been brought up to think that women were fragile creatures whom he had nothing in common with, it wasn't surprising that he wasn't ready to deal with one who could beat him at his own game and be a friend to share jokes with at the same time.

Well, Rick Hendricks was changing his attitude about girls—just as Joanna de Mayo was changing hers about boys. I guess being in love can do that!

Chapter Eleven

It seemed as if meeting Rick was the cue for all sorts of good things to start happening. One good thing that threw my family into complete chaos was Greg's announcement.

Rick, who seemed to be in permanent residence at our house these days, was with me the Saturday afternoon Greg's letter arrived. Actually, Rick and I had just come back, exhausted but triumphant, from our tennis match, in which we had won every single game. We met the mailman at the front gate, so we were the ones who brought in the letter.

"Look what's just come from Greg," I called, waving it around as we entered the family room. My father and Martin were watching car races on TV. The drapes were drawn, and it was like stepping into a cave. "Here," I said, dropping the letter onto my father's lap. "I'll pull back the drapes. You can't read anything in this light."

"Hey!" Martin said irritably. "Two cars almost crashed."

"Bloodthirsty creep," I said. "Go ahead, Dad, read Greg's letter."

"Well, I must say this is a change," said my father, opening it slowly. "He's been calling and reversing the charges lately. I wonder why he's suddenly found time to put pen to paper again."

"Probably needs some money," said Peter, coming in from the kitchen with a sandwich piled about four inches high. "How did you guys do this morning?"

"Creamed them," I said. "It was a boring match."

"Listen to her," said Martin, trying to help himself to half of Peter's sandwich. "She's getting so big-headed she will only want to play with Bjorn Borg soon."

"Good heavens!" said my father, so loudly and suddenly that we all stopped and looked at him.

"Is it bad news from Greg?" I asked.

"I don't know if it's bad or good, but it's certainly news," my father said. "Hey, Margie, get in here. Big news from Greg!"

"News from Greg—what's wrong?" asked Mother from the door.

"I think I'd better read it out loud," said my father. (Sometimes he drives us all crazy with his patience.) "'Now for the surprise of the century,' Greg says." He adjusted his glasses. "'Your playboy son has decided to settle down and become respectable. I've asked Hanni Weibl to marry me, and she has said yes.'"

"Hanni Weibl!" we all exclaimed. Hanni Weibl was just about the hottest item around in women's tennis.

"Go on, dear," said my mother, trying to peer over his shoulder.

"'We want to get married next month. Since Hanni's folks are all in Austria, we thought it would be nice to have the wedding at our place.'"

"He wants a wedding here—next month?" my mother exploded. "I hope he doesn't want a big fancy wedding."

"'We don't want a big wedding,'" my father read, smiling. "'Just to be married quietly with a few close friends and the family. I'll be flying up soon to plan the details with you.'"

When he finished the letter, we all just stared at one another for a while.

Then my father said quietly, "I hope he knows what he's doing. She doesn't look to me like the kind of woman who will want to settle down and darn somebody's socks."

Greg arrived the next week, looking chic and sophisticated—as the future husband of an international tennis star should look. It soon became obvious that his version of a quiet wedding for close friends and the family would involve around two hundred people, and he wanted to have it in the garden so that the press photographers could get good pictures. Furthermore, we found out that Hanni's family also expected to take part. Greg announced casually that her parents, plus little sister Trudi, plus Hanni's grandmother, would all be flying over for the wedding.

"That's nice, dear," said my mother. "We'll arrange rooms for them at the Holiday Inn."

"Holiday Inn?" Greg asked in amazement. "But I told them they could stay with us."

"Stay with us?" shrieked my mother. "You want me to turn my backyard into a classic rose garden, arrange food and drink for two hundred, be invaded by every newspaper in the country, and have four Austrians as houseguests? Really, Greg—there are limits!"

"I don't see any big problem," said Greg, looking offended. "Martin can sleep on the couch in the family room, and Peter can sleep out on the porch, and we have two camp cots somewhere. And Hanni can share with Jo."

"I don't see why I have to sleep on the porch!" Peter complained. "What if it rains? I'll catch pneumonia. Let Greg sleep on the porch if he wants guests in the house."

"It's my wedding," Greg said. "It's important I don't catch pneumonia."

The day before Hanni's family was due to arrive (Hanni was playing in a tournament in Houston and wouldn't get here for two more days), everything was in a turmoil. My mother was flicking through cookbooks to find a recipe for apple strudel, Martin was walking around with a German dictionary muttering, *"Guten Tag, wie geht es Ihnen?"* and Peter and my father were up in the attic, yelling out occasional curses as they tried to find the camp cots under piles of junk.

Rick and I did the only sensible thing. We got out in a hurry.

"Whew," Rick sighed, as we were safely out of sight. "I've learned one thing from this. When I get married, I'm going to slip away without telling anyone. If your family, who're usually so easygoing, crack up under the pressure, can you imagine what mine would do?"

We walked down the hill in contented silence.

"Where do you want to go?" Rick asked as

we crossed the bridge. There hadn't been much rain that spring, and the river below had shrunk to a brown trickle moving sluggishly between mud flats.

"I don't care," I said, looking down at the water. Then I had an idea. "I know! Let's take a picnic to Piper Park. It's nice and peaceful there."

"But we haven't got any food."

"We could stop at the deli and get a couple of submarine sandwiches. I'll treat—I'm feeling rich this week."

"You don't have to do that," Rick said, looking a little annoyed. "I have money on me." The chauvinist in him still crept out at times.

"Look, stubborn," I said, taking his face in my hands, "I made a lot of money babysitting those awful kids across the street last night, and I want to treat. Can you get that into your thick head?"

Then he kissed me quickly and said I was a domineering woman, but he let me buy the sandwiches.

"Off on a picnic, are you?" asked old Mrs. Garetzki behind the counter. "Lovely day to be in the fresh air."

"We thought we'd go up to Piper Park," Rick said.

"Oh, Piper Park. It's lovely there at this time

of year. When Mr. Garetzki was alive, we used to go walking there every Sunday. Enjoy yourselves." She smiled as she handed us the lunch.

We headed back to the river, then followed the path along the bank until we came to the sign announcing the park. It seemed totally deserted, and we found a heavenly spot under a big oak. The stream was more lively here, and it splashed its way between big moss-covered rocks. Dragonflies, bright green or red, flitted like miniature helicopters over the surface, and once a kingfisher skimmed past as a bright flash of blue.

I kicked off my thongs and lowered my feet into the cool water. "Isn't this fantastic?" I sighed.

"Hey, young lady, don't just sit there doing nothing," Rick said in a commanding voice. "I want my lunch. Come up here and attend to the needs of your lord and master."

I was there in a flash, but not to serve him lunch. "Listen here, you chauvinist pig," I said, wrestling him to the ground. "You will never be my lord and master—understand?"

"We'll see about that," he said, freeing himself with one strong move and crushing me beneath him as he rolled over, pinning me to the ground.

My arms were trapped by my sides. His lips were a fraction of an inch above mine.

"Do you surrender now?" he asked.

"If I surrender, can I have my lunch?" I teased. "I'm starving."

"You may have your lunch if you agree that I'm your lord and master."

"I'd rather die of starvation."

"Your trouble is that you are just as stubborn as I am," he said, laughing. Then he kissed me. Lunch was forgotten for quite a while after that.

When we finally ate, it was delicious—crisp French rolls with just the right amount of meat, cheese, tomatoes, and pickles. Rick crumpled up his wrapper and stuffed it into his pocket, then leaned his back against the big oak tree. "I feel very content," he said.

"Me, too," I agreed and came to lean against his shoulder. "It's so peaceful here."

"Rick! Hey, Rick!" The shout cut through the afternoon peace like a power saw through timber. We both sat up, startled. Two figures were rushing down the track toward us, waving and yelling, "Hey, Rick!"

Rick sighed deeply. "Guess who? How on earth did my sisters manage to track us down here? Do you think we could make a run for it?"

120

But before we could scramble to our feet, they closed in, panting and giggling.

"How the devil did you find us?" Rick grumbled.

"We just happened to be in the deli, and Mrs. Garetzki said that she had seen you."

"Jo and I would like to be alone this afternoon," he said. There was an edge to his voice.

"Oh, we know that," said Trisha, the youngest and prettiest, "but you can't be alone this afternoon. Not after you promised."

"Promised what?"

"Don't tell me you've forgotten already," she said, pouting. "Serena went with all her friends, and you promised you'd take us."

"Take you where?"

"To the fair, of course. Don't you remember? When Serena said she was going with the Aliotos, Mom said we could go only if you took us."

"Oh, that." Rick sighed. He got to his feet wearily. "That's right. I did promise."

I usually tried to be understanding about the responsibility Rick felt for his sisters, but sometimes they really took advantage of him. Secretly, I thought the best thing he could do for them was make them stand on their own two feet once in a while instead of always letting them rely on him. Of course, I never said that to him. But I was so disappointed at having our afternoon spoiled that I said sulkily, "Can't you go tomorrow?"

"No, I wouldn't dream of it," said Rick, pulling me up and looking cheerful again. "I promised to do it this afternoon, and we are going to do it this afternoon!" As the two girls walked on ahead of him, he whispered to me, "Don't worry. I think this might be the last interruption from my sisters for a long time."

I didn't know what he had up his sleeve, but he seemed very cheerful, so, after one quick backward glance at our beautiful picnic spot, I plodded after him.

When his sisters were far enough ahead, I grabbed his arm. "OK, what's the plan? You have that wild, wicked look in your eye."

He grinned. "We are going to the fair, and we are going to go on all the rides. My sisters have very weak stomachs. Maybe we can teach them a lesson."

We walked back to my house and piled into Rick's car. The fair was about ten miles away. It wasn't as big as the one in the fall, but it did have a carnival. When we got there, we parked the car, and then Rick headed straight to the midway. "Come on, you slowpokes, we want to make sure we don't miss any of the rides," he said heartily. "Come on, Alison, you go on the Sonic Whirl with me, and Trisha can go with Jo."

After three rides Rick and I were enjoying ourselves. We both loved speed, and the rides were very fast. Then Rick bought us all ice cream cones, and we went on the Moon Rocket. I thought Trisha looked decidedly green when we got off.

"I think we should have a rest from rides now," Alison said. "I want you to win me a teddy bear, Rick."

"Oh, come on, don't be such spoilsports," Rick said, grabbing her arm. "Teddy bears are boring. I took you to the fair, didn't I? You don't want to stand around watching me throw balls at milk bottles." And he led her very firmly toward the Whip.

After the Whip I bought us all hot dogs and made sure the vendor went heavy on the catsup, mustard, and pickles.

"I think I'd like to go home now," Trisha said. "I need to wash my hair tonight."

"Wash your hair?" Rick asked. "I didn't drive all this way and fight for a parking space just to spend a few minutes here. We haven't been on nearly everything yet." And so it went until it got late.

The girls were very silent all the way home, and when Rick said that he had had such a good time that he would take them back again the next day, Alison found that she had too much homework and Trisha said that she had hurt her back on the Whip and couldn't go anywhere.

Outside Rick exploded with, "I think we won! Maybe next time they'll think twice before asking someone else to entertain them!"

Chapter Twelve

The next morning Hanni's family arrived. Dad and Greg had driven to Logan to meet their plane, and my mother stayed home, rushing around to reinspect their rooms and to double-check the menus. When Dad returned, he drove up the drive honking. I watched from my window as they all climbed out of our old VW bus.

Hanni's mother was an enormous mountain of a woman, with braids piled up on top of her head, and I could see instantly that she liked giving orders. Hanni's father was a small, fragile-looking man with a gray, wispy mustache, and he looked a little frightened of his giant of a wife. Hanni's sister was plump and blonde, like something out of a travel poster, and the grandmother was an older, slightly more fierce-looking version of her mother.

They spoke almost no English except for

Trudi, who had taken it in high school and knew such useful things as, "All the rivers are frozen over," and "The train is standing on platform four." They looked with suspicion at Mother's carefully prepared Austrian menu, and Hanni's mother poked the apple strudel with her fork, asking "Vat is zis?"

That first day was pretty tense for all of us, so it was with many misgivings that we waited for Hanni's arrival. I was sure she would be a cross between her mother and the typical superstar. She would probably take one look at my room and turn up her beautiful nose. "You vant me to share zis dump mit her?" she would ask, and then she would change all the wedding arrangements, from the menu to the music.

I was helping my mother with a last minute cleanup (our house had never been so clean for so long before!) when there was a ring at the front door.

"Get that, will you, Jo?" my mother asked. A young blonde woman stood there, dressed in old, faded jeans, a T-shirt, and clogs. She grinned at me and looked so familiar that I wondered if she was one of Greg's old girl-friends come to say a final farewell.

"Hi," I said. "Can I help you?"

She laughed then. "I am Hanni," she said, "and you are Joanna."

"Hanni?" I said, trying to reconcile this ordinary woman with the glamorous super-star I had seen on TV.

She laughed again. "I always travel like this—that way no one recognizes me."

"But Greg has gone to the airport to meet you," I said. "We thought you were arriving at noon."

"Oh, he must be furious, waiting at the airport," she said. "I was too impatient, I guess. There was an early flight today, by way of Atlanta, so I took it. I thought I would surprise you all."

"Well, you'd better come in and call to let him know you're here," I said and picked up her one suitcase.

Hanni turned out, contrary to all our worst fears, to be quite wonderful. She was bouncy and friendly, and pretty soon my brothers were following her around, waiting for her every command. We also liked her because she was not afraid of her mother, no matter how much she commanded, blustered, and criticized. Hanni only laughed and did what she wanted anyway. She was happy with all the wedding plans and asked Trudi and me to be her bridesmaids. I think a few months ago I would have refused to be anyone's bridesmaid and wear a frilly dress, but now I felt excited as I drove into town with Hanni and Trudi and we picked two gorgeous pale lilac dresses with shoes to match and ordered real pink and lilac flowers for our hair.

"How's the wedding coming along?" Rick asked every time he saw me. He was invited, and I was looking forward to seeing him in a suit for the first time.

"Everything's going so smoothly that it's too good to be true," I answered. "Hanni's mother wanted to change the whole order of the ceremony, and she didn't like any of the food we'd planned, but Hanni just told her nothing could be changed now."

The wedding was only three days away. The press had already got wind of it, and we had been bothered by several people creeping around our garden. Hanni had done an official interview for some women's magazine, and both she and Greg had been on the local morning TV talk show. All sorts of famous tennis players and celebrity friends of Hanni's had promised to come.

"You won't stand a chance when I meet all these gorgeous men," I teased Rick.

"Ha!" he said. "Have you thought that there might be some pretty cute girls there, too? A lot of these celebrities prefer younger men!"

Late that evening we all sat out in the garden and talked. My mother had worked miracles, and the roses were trained into beautiful arches. Their scent was sweet and heavy in the darkness.

"Only three more days, and you'll be Mrs. Greg de Mayo," Greg said, patting Hanni's knee. She smiled at him.

"To you—yes," she said. "But I won't be giving up my own name. After all, I couldn't call myself Hanni Weibl-de Mayo in tournaments, could I?"

"The umpires would certainly choke on that." My father laughed.

"Where are you two going for your honeymoon—or is it a secret?" Peter asked.

"Hawaii," said Greg. "France," said Hanni at the same time. They both stopped short and looked at each other.

"What do you mean, Hawaii?" Hanni asked, an edge to her voice. "I have to play in the French Open. I assumed that was the more important tournament, and you wouldn't want me to miss it."

"But, Hanni, I have to play in Hawaii—it's a big purse, and you couldn't want a better place for a honeymoon. I thought we agreed that Hawaii would be an ideal honeymoon for us."

"Yes, but that was when we were just talking things over in theory. Not after we had set the date. You knew I had the French Open coming up, and you know how important it is to me."

"But Hawaii is really important to me," Greg said. "And we already made the plans. With most of the top players out of the way in Europe, I have a good chance—"

"This top player will be out of the way in Europe, too," Hanni said icily.

"Come on, you two," my father said. "Surely you can come to a compromise on this—delay your honeymoon for a couple of weeks."

"It is not just that," Hanni said, in her precise English. She had risen to her feet and looked very angry. "It is a question of whose career comes first—his or mine. The way he assumed, without even asking me, that I would give up the French Open to go to Hawaii with him . . ."

She shook her head. "I'm sorry, Greg. I'm just not about to become a meek little housewife trailing around behind her husband. You know that."

"Of course I know it, Hanni—and I do respect your career," he said. "But I just thought one tournament for our honeymoon is not much to ask you to give up."

"It is too much," Hanni said, and she ran toward the house.

The rest of us sat in stunned silence. Later

I walked to the house beside Greg. He shook his head. "She just doesn't understand. I do care about her career. It's just that I don't want to be thought of as Hanni Weibl's husband. I want to make it, too. I don't want people to say that she makes all the money, and we live in her apartment—" He broke off then and hurried to his room.

The next morning nobody knew what to do. Nobody wanted to cancel all the arrangements and get rid of all the reporters. I certainly didn't want to take back my lilac dress. We were a little anxious to get rid of Hanni's family, for they seemed to think we were entirely to blame for the wedding plans falling through. But unfortunately, they had already booked their flight back and couldn't get an earlier one, so we were all stuck with one another a few days more.

It was all very depressing. I needed to think, so I climbed up my treehouse. It was only when I reached the platform that I saw I was not alone. Hanni was already up there, staring out into the distance.

"You must all hate me," she said.

"Of course we don't hate you," I said. "We understand how you feel."

"Why am I so stubborn?" she asked.

"Greg is stubborn, too. We're a stubborn family."

"It sounds like such a little thing to quarrel over," she said. "You all think I am stupid, that I am making a fuss over nothing. But to me it is not little. You are probably thinking, what is one tournament? And I agree with that. But my career is so important. I have worked hard to get where I am—and now it will always be my tournament or his tournament, deciding which is more important. I cannot give in to Greg all the time. I know that now."

"Then it's good that you found it out before you got married," I said. "Maybe you should marry someone who can follow your career."

But she shook her head, and a tear appeared on her cheek. "But I love Greg. He is the only one I have ever loved. I want to marry him, but I do not want to stop being Hanni Weibl, either."

"I don't think Greg wants you to," I said. "But I think I know why he wants to go to Hawaii so badly. You're already a top player. Everyone has heard of you. You make lots of money, and you win tournaments. Greg's still only a newcomer. He'd like to prove that he can make it, too. He doesn't like the thought of your earning more money than he does—and this Hawaiian tournament would even you up a little bit."

She looked at me, then said, "Yes, I understand. I think you are right. Of course, you are right. Maybe I have been thinking only of myself and not about Greg, too."

With a determined look, she climbed down the steps and headed toward the house. By midday the wedding was on again. Greg and Hanni must have had a good long talk because now they seemed happier than ever. They came close to another fight when Greg announced that they would go to France for their honeymoon. "No—to Hawaii," Hanni said. But then they saw the funny side, and both laughed it off.

"People fight over the stupidest things," Rick said when I told him about it.

"Not really," I said. "The thing that starts the fight might seem to be trivial, but there is usually something bigger behind it."

"Listen to Miss Philosophy!" Rick said in admiration. "Anyway, we will never fight over stupid things, will we?"

"Never," I said. "We're much too sensible for that."

Then I thought a little. "But remind me never to marry a tennis player," I said. "I couldn't stand that constant fighting over whose tournament to go to."

"That's all right, then," said Rick, "because I am going to be a computer expert."

That sentence, and how Rick said it, made

me feel really good. It was like watching the future unfolding in front of me like a long red carpet!

The wedding went without a hitch. Hanni was a radiant bride, Greg a handsome groom, and everybody told me I was a lovely bridesmaid, too. We all got used to having everything we did photographed, and Hanni's mother was even seen to smile more than once and said she had had a "vonderful time."

Then the happy couple left on their wedding trip—to Bermuda. They had decided to give up both their tournaments and spend a couple of weeks away from it all. I thought it was fantastic—like a romantic fairy tale come true. I couldn't help having a few daydreams about my wedding—in which Rick, or someone looking remarkably like him, also figured.

Chapter Thirteen

Another good by-product of being a twosome with Rick was that I had more in common with other girls. Now that I was known as half of Rick and Joanna, I found myself invited to all the things I had only heard about secondhand before—things like swim parties, barbecues, and double dates to movies ending with visits to the ice cream parlor. Now, instead of getting defensive and changing the subject or sitting in sullen silence when Dee Dee or the others talked about their dates at lunchtime, I actually listened with interest. I still thought they went overboard with their preoccupation with the subject—especially Angie, who didn't seem to care about anything else—but I was really beginning to enjoy being with them again.

My family started to complain that they never saw me at home anymore. "Pardon me, ma'am, but I think you're in the wrong house," Martin said when I arrived home late one night. "This is the de Mayo residence. Two parents, three brothers, and one dog. There used to be one sister, too, but she vanished a while back!"

But my mother was glad for me and told me how well I was looking. "I told you so, didn't I?" she said, a twinkle in her eye. "I knew it was going to happen sooner or later."

Another thing that made her happy was that, after all those years, she had a real live daughter at last. It meant she could do all the things I had denied her up till now, like going on shopping trips to choose clothes. With my social life suddenly in a whirl, I discovered that I owned no clothes to wear to parties or on dates. My mother was only too happy to help me choose some, but she required a little education. "Mom, nobody wears dresses to parties anymore, and certainly not frilly dresses like that. Couldn't I just have a pair of white jeans instead?"

We got the white jeans. That evening I admired myself in the mirror. The new jeans, which my mother claimed were a size too small for me, looked as if they were molded to my skin. I had chosen a pretty peach-color silky blouse to go with them. To finish off the effect, I went down to the garden and picked a pale peach rose to wear in my hair.

"Hey!" Rick said, looking very approving as I made my dramatic entrance down the stairs. "I'm going to keep you trapped in a corner somewhere so that the other guys don't come and steal you away."

But it didn't turn out like that at all. Quite the opposite, in fact.

The party was at Scott McKinley's house. From the way Scott looked at me as we walked in, I could tell that he no longer thought of me as a former female football player or "only de Mayo." Even Artie was too speechless to say anything for once. He just stood and stared at me with his mouth open.

The party was a barbecue in Scott's back-yard. Lanterns were strung among the trees, and kids were dancing on the patio. We could smell the delicious scent of spareribs cooking.

"Come on, let's get something to drink before we start dancing," Rick said and took my hand.

But we never made it to the punch bowl.

"Well, Joanna, fancy seeing you here!" drawled a voice, and there was Angie, looking gorgeous in a white lace-trimmed long dress, smiling at me sweetly. (She had the most remarkable ability to turn into a completely

different person when boys were around!)
Then she pretended to notice Rick for the
first time. "And is this the gorgeous guy I've
been hearing about?"

Reluctantly I introduced them. "Angie, this
is Rick Hendricks. Rick, this is Angie Peterson."

"Hi," Rick said in an offhanded sort of
way.

"Hi!" she breathed, making it sound like an
imitation of Marilyn Monroe in one of those
old sexy movies. "Joanna and I are old, old
friends, but we don't see enough of each
other these days." She smiled, and I wondered
if Rick could guess that we could barely stand
the sight of each other.

I couldn't help smiling, though. She was so
obviously making a play for Rick that I felt
sure any self-respecting boy must see
through it. I glanced at him, and he winked,
making me feel a lot better.

Then Angie ignored me and turned her full
charm on him. "You're not a sophomore, are
you? You look much too mature to be a sophomore."

"No," he said very seriously, "I'm still in
junior high actually. I was kept back three
years."

"Oh . . ." She looked confused and disappointed and drifted away.

I was shaking with held-back laughter. Rick saw my face and started laughing, too.

"Well, she deserved it," he said. "She was coming on too strong."

"But you have to admit she's cute," I said.

He shrugged his shoulders. "If you like that sort of thing."

We had a good time, eating, drinking, and dancing. Then, later in the evening, Angie appeared again.

"You are a very wicked person, Rick Hendricks," she said very severely. "I've just been talking to a guy on the tennis team, and I find out that you're a junior! It's not nice to tell lies. Didn't your mother ever tell you that?"

Rick laughed and put an arm around me. "She said it was OK in self-defense," he said and led me away. As we walked across the patio, I saw Scott standing in the shadows, watching Angie. His face was a picture of misery.

I thought Rick had been rude enough to Angie to crush her hopes forever, but the next day at school Scott grabbed me as I walked alone down the hall.

"Listen, I have to talk to you."

He sounded so dramatic that I stopped.

"It's about Angie. She's after Rick."

"That's pretty obvious."

"But you know Angie. She won't give up when she wants something. She goes on and on until she gets it."

"Look, Scott, I'm not worried, and I don't think you should be. Rick was only amused by her. He teased her all last night. In fact, he was pretty rude to her."

"But that will make her all the more eager. You know what she's like—only child, very spoiled, always had everything she asked for. If she doesn't get something right away, that makes it all the more interesting. And I tell you, she wants Rick. She won't give up until she's got him."

"Well, she's going to have to fight me for him first, and, as you should well know, Scott McKinley, I punch a lot harder than she does."

I thought that would make Scott smile, but he only sighed. "The trouble is that people like Angie get what they want by acting helpless. She's very clever at it—and at being in the right place at the right time. In the end it usually works for her. You're a normal person, not some dumb featherbrain, Joanna, and I just wanted to warn you."

I patted his arm, something I would never have dreamed of doing before, but which now felt quite natural. "Don't worry, Scott. You're not going to lose Angie, and she's not going to get Rick. We tough guys have got to stick together."

"Yeah." He smiled weakly and uncertainly and walked away.

Over the next few days I saw what he meant. Angie certainly was persistent, I had to give her that. She showed up at the end of tennis practice to walk me home, "just like the good old days," as she put it. Unfortunately for her, Rick had a dentist's appointment in town that day, so we two girls walked home together, saying one thing and meaning another all the way up the hill.

"Do you remember the old treehouse," she said nostalgically, "and the games we used to play up there and all your jokes? Do you remember when you tipped that pitcher of Kool-Aid over me last summer? Wasn't that hysterically funny? I thought we would never stop laughing."

"Yes," I said quietly, "I remember it well."

"We had such fun in those days, didn't we, Joanna?" she asked sweetly. "I do hope we can see more of each other now. I've been keeping out of circulation too long, going with Scottie. You know, it's not good to keep yourself tied to one boy at our age. You get out of the swing of things. You don't meet enough people. To be honest with you, I'm getting tired of Scottie. I need a change."

Well, I thought, you are not getting back into the swing of things with my Rick, or you'll get more than Kool-Aid over your head next time.

"I have to rush, Angie," I said out loud. "Thanks for coming by to walk me home. Let's do it again." Although all the words were right, there was no way Angie could have missed the real meaning. Her real motives were so obvious, and while I'd try to be polite, there was no way I could be friendly to this former best friend who had turned into a person I didn't know, or like, at all.

I told Dee Dee on the phone that night what had happened, and, as usual, she tried to play referee and see both sides. "Don't be too hard on her, Jo. I know she can be impossible around boys, but she'll get over it one day."

"I sure hope it's soon," I answered, "because I'll never be as tolerant and understanding as you are about that sort of thing!"

Dee Dee laughed and said, "But at least you're giving it a good try now. You've come a long way, kid."

A couple of days later Angie showed up after dinner at my house. This time she was either lucky, or she had done some snooping, because Rick was there. Her eyes lit up like a spider with a fly already trapped in her web.

"Oh, I'm sorry," she cooed. "I didn't know you had company." She paused to smile her toothpaste commercial smile in his direction and said, "Hi, Rick," then turned back to me. "Silly me—I left my math book at school. You don't happen to be through with yours, do you?"

"My math book?" We weren't in any of the same classes, so she clearly had done a lot of research to find out what homework I might have tonight. I walked across to my backpack and took out the book. "Sure. I'm through with it," I said, and I handed it to her.

She flicked through it. "Ugh. I hate algebra. I can never quite get the hang of it. Are you good at algebra, Rick?"

"Not me," he said. "I got a D in algebra. Mr. Abbott was going to flunk me, but he said my papers were so nice and neat that he gave me a D for effort."

"Oh." Angie's face fell. She had clearly planned a cozy evening, sitting next to Rick on my sofa, gazing up at him adoringly while he did her algebra for her.

"Oh, well," she said at last, "I guess I better be going then. It's going to take me positively hours to get through this math."

Rick and I said nothing.

"I can see myself sitting up past midnight," she went on. "I'd better go, or I'll never finish. Thank you for the book, Joanna. Bye, Rick." Then she swept out.

As the door closed, we both exploded into laughter.

"You know, you are really terrible," I said. "You got an A in algebra."

"Well, you didn't want me to volunteer to do her homework, did you?" he said. "That was what she wanted, wasn't it? Did you want to have her here all evening? If so, I can call her back. . . ."

"Don't you dare."

"Well, then, remember, all's fair in love and war."

I snuggled up to his shoulder. After a while he gave a little laugh again. "Angie," he said, "just does not give up. Do you think she's going to haunt us for the rest of our lives?"

It certainly began to look that way. At the tennis match on Saturday she was in the crowd, cheering. She appeared from nowhere while we were eating our lunch on the grass, and then we heard that she had switched her P.E. class to tennis so that Rick could help her with her strokes.

Scott had been right about one thing. She certainly didn't give up.

Chapter Fourteen

Angie was continuing her Catch-a-Rick campaign. I admired her persistence, but I was secure in my knowledge that Rick wanted me. Then the end of the school year was approaching—seniors rushed around muttering about graduation dresses, hairstyles, corsages, and partners for the prom. We lesser beings still had our own high spots to look forward to, however. First, there was the High School Cup, which Rick and I were to compete in. Then, my family had rented a beach cottage at Cape Cod for the summer, and, wonder of wonders, they had said I could invite Rick to spend two weeks there with us. I was counting off the days, going into long daydreams about strolling hand in hand with him down moonlit beaches with gentle waves breaking and sighing and the moonlight shining across the water. So, my thoughts were not too much on the tennis cup until

Coach Parker gave us a pep talk in his office one afternoon.

"Well, guys, we've had a good season. We've only lost two matches, and I'm proud of you. Joanna, I'm especially proud of you—you haven't lost a game all spring . . . but now comes the big one. It's less than three weeks to the State Cup, and I want all of you to start psyching yourselves up for it. I say all of you, and I mean all of you. Of course, I plan to have Rick and Jo play the doubles in the A division, but if one of them were to break a leg or come down with the flu or something—and let me add that I will personally murder them if they do—I want Tony and Bill to be prepared to take their places. Understood?"

"Yes, Coach," we all said in unison like kindergartners.

"So get out there and start playing. You're not playing singles anymore, remember that. You've got to think as a team, to cover for each other, anticipate each other's moves, back each other up. I don't want to see two stars out there, each trying to score the winning point—I want to see a twosome. OK, get playing."

We walked out toward the court. It had been raining the day before, and the air was still heavy and humid. Not the sort of day you want to run about on a tennis court. Rick and I immediately got into an argument over who was going to play where. The trouble was that we were both strong forehand players, both right-handed, and we both wanted to play on the forehand court. After a little arguing and shuffling around, I finally agreed—because Coach Parker had ordered me to—to play the backhand court.

"Now, Joanna, stop pouting," he ordered. "You know that your backhand is stronger than Rick's, and you can cover the center of the court with your forehand, too."

"If you don't think I'm good enough for you, why don't you just slice yourself down the middle and play both halves of the court yourself," said Rick, who was also edgy that afternoon. Normally I would have laughed at that, but instead, I paced over to my side of the court and ignored him.

The heat was irritating. It had brought out the mosquitoes, who zoomed in to land on our sticky skin, and we couldn't take our eyes off the ball to stop and slap them. After we had played for a while, one thing became obvious. Tony and Bill, who had played together as a doubles team all spring, certainly knew how to play as a team, and we didn't. They would open us up and then send the ball between us. We both began to get more and more bad-tempered. Then finally Tony sent a beautiful shot right down the center line between us. Rick and I both stood like dummies and glowered at each other.

"That was your ball," Rick said accusingly. "Remember what Coach said about your fabulous forehand that is meant to cover the middle of the court."

"Not when the ball is definitely on your side," I said. "I wouldn't want to be accused of poaching your shots."

"The ball was not on my side," said Rick. "It was right in the center, and I didn't want to risk missing it with my inferior backhand."

"Well, I'm glad you've finally realized the limits of your capabilities," I shouted. "If Coach had let me play on the forehand court where I wanted to play, we wouldn't have missed that shot."

"Well, isn't that a typical female comment—make a mistake and then blame it on someone else!"

"I'm hardly going to take the blame for *your* mistake, am I?" I yelled. "In the future maybe I should yell at you when it's your turn to hit the ball!"

"I've had enough of being yelled at," Rick said. "If there's one thing I can't stand, it's pushy women."

"Well, if that's how you feel, I'm sure there are girls around who'd be happy to let you be as macho as you think you are! In fact, I know one who's dying for a date with you."

"Good idea," Rick said. "It will make a change to go out with a real girl again!" He stalked off the court.

The three of us who were left just stood there in embarrassed silence. I was determined not to cry in front of Tony and Bill, and I blinked back the tears as I put on my racket cover. They came over to me.

"You're an idiot, Jo," Tony said. "You know what a temper he has and how touchy he is about his tennis. You shouldn't have goaded him like that."

"I don't need you to make things worse," I snapped and turned away.

Bill caught up with me and took my arm. "Jo, would you like me to walk home with you?" he asked.

I shook my head, managed to mumble, "No, thanks," and ran on.

I ran all the way home, all the way upstairs, and collapsed onto my bed. Then I let the tears come. I cried for about half an hour, and then, when there were no more tears left, I lay and stared at the ceiling and tried to think what had happened.

Had I lost Rick forever? Surely it couldn't be as bad as all that. We had fights sometimes. We snapped at each other, then we got over it in a few minutes. We both had quick tempers, but we both got it out of our systems quickly, too. Once he had calmed down he would realize we had both been stupid, and he would come back. Perhaps we would even both laugh over it. After all, missing a ball was a stupid thing to fight over, wasn't it?

Then I remembered the talk with Hanni in the treehouse and thought how much easier it was to analyze other people's relationships than one's own. Was this fight only over missing a ball, or was it about Rick's still not completely accepting a girl as an equal on the tennis court?

Maybe (I thought of Hanni again) it happened because I was only thinking of myself. Or just maybe the real fight was about both things.

I splashed cold water into my eyes and came down to supper. If the family noticed anything odd about me, they were nice enough not to mention it. I left the dining room door open and waited for Rick to call. He didn't call all through dinner. After dinner I got undressed and brushed my hair, still listening for the phone.

I sent out frantic thought waves to him. Come on, Rick. You know you were stupid this afternoon. When that didn't work, I started giving mental orders to the phone: ring, phone, ring. I command you to ring right now. Please ring before I go to bed. . . .

Then the phone did ring. I streaked down the stairs two at a time, but it was only someone wanting to talk to my father.

Well, I suppose he needs to sleep on it first, I thought. Tomorrow everything will be all right again.

I didn't see Rick all morning. Then in chemistry class, a girl I knew slightly, who was going with one of Rick's friends, came over to my seat. "Hey, what's with you and Rick—is it all over?" she asked.

"Why?" I asked. I had a horrible sinking feeling.

"Well, he was at the Pizza Palace last night with a different girl. Angie something or other. She kept gazing up at him all evening, and he looked as if he was enjoying it."

Even then I didn't quite believe her. Rick must have put her up to saying that, I thought. It was one of his sick jokes. He just wanted to pay me back and make me jealous. Of course he wouldn't take Angie to the Pizza Palace, I told myself. He thinks she's a big pain. . . .

I half expected to see him laughing at me as

I showed up for tennis practice after school. "I fooled you, didn't I?" he would say. "I had you worried for a moment there?"

But Rick wasn't at tennis practice.

"I'm sorry, Jo," Tony said. "He said he was going to skip practice today, and he walked home with some girl."

Now, at last, I believed. I had lost him. Forever.

Chapter Fifteen

When I was nine years old, our cat got run over. I remember seeing her body lying beside the road, all hunched over, as if trying to protect herself from death. I thought that the pain of that day was more than I could bear. I thought I would never get over it. I felt that my heart, literally, would just break into pieces.

But no pain I had ever felt in my whole life was equal to the one I felt now that I had lost Rick. I went over that fight again and again in my mind—punishing myself for the stupid, spiteful things I said, for how I had hurt him. How could I have been so dumb? Why did I fly off the handle and say things without thinking?

No one, boy or girl, likes to be told he is no good at his favorite sport. And for Rick, who still wasn't too sure how he felt about competing with his girlfriend, it was the final straw to be humiliated in front of his friends. No wonder he chose Angie—quiet little Angie, who'd had years of practice in playing up to boys, knowing when to flatter them and how to make them feel strong. Now I had lost everything that mattered, my tennis as well as Rick, because he and I could never be partners in the State Cup, never play on the same team next year. . . .

At home I managed to act fairly normal. I didn't want to have to answer a whole lot of questions, and I didn't want their pity, either. So I came to meals on time, did my chores, spoke when spoken to, and made myself look presentable every morning.

But of course questions were bound to arise in the end.

"Where's the famous Rick these days?" Peter asked at dinner one night. "We haven't seen him for ages. Don't tell me he got tired of our cooking?"

"Yeah, what happened?" Martin wanted to know. "Did you two have a fight?"

"Why don't you shut up and mind your own business," I said. "I don't want to talk about it." Then I rushed out to the kitchen, that very kitchen where he had kissed me with a face full of soapsuds, and stood staring at the sink. I didn't even hear my mother come in behind me.

"Is that what's wrong?" she asked. "You've broken up with Rick?"

I spun on her fiercely. "Yes, and it's all your fault," I said. "If I hadn't inherited this bad temper from somebody, we would never have fought in the first place."

My mother was used to having unusual accusations flung at her. She smiled at me, understanding how I felt. "Don't take it too hard, darling," she said. "After all, you are going to date lots of boys before you find the special one you're going to marry. And every time you split up with one of them, it is going to hurt a little."

"A little?" I yelled. "Why didn't you tell me before I started how much it would hurt? I would never have let myself fall in love with anyone if I had known. I can't believe anything could hurt that much."

Then my mother came over to me and put both arms around me. "Oh, honey," she said, patting me on the back as if I were a baby again. "I know it's hard. I know it hurts, but you'll get over it soon. Believe me. . . ."

Her arms around me were too much for my defenses. I felt the tears come streaming down my cheeks. I put my head on her shoulder, and she stroked my hair.

"I won't get over it ever," I sobbed. "I'll love him till the day I die."

My mother let me cry and cry, although her shoulder must have been getting pretty wet. Then she grabbed a towel and dried my tears. "Now try to cheer up. It might not be as bad as all that. One quarrel doesn't mean a relationship is finished. I bet after a while Rick will start missing you. . . ."

"No he won't. He's already found someone much better for him than me."

"Then you'll have to make him jealous. Go out with another boy yourself."

"It's taken me fifteen years to get the first one," I said, starting to cry again. "I don't think he'll be around when I turn thirty."

My mother laughed.

"It's not funny," I snapped.

She tried to stop smiling. "No, honey, I know it's not. But I'm sure it will be all right in the end, and one day you'll be able to laugh about it, too."

I thought again about what she said the next day when Scott McKinley joined me in the cafeteria. He looked about as down as I felt, and I felt sorry for him.

"Mind if I sit here?" he asked.

"Go ahead. It's a free country."

"How you feeling?"

"Terrible."

"Me, too."

We both ate for a while in silence. Then he said, "It's no good sitting here feeling depressed. We can't spend our whole lives feeling sorry for ourselves. We ought to do something to get us out of our depression."

"Like what?"

"Oh, I don't know. There must be something. We could go to a funny movie. Yeah, that would be a good idea, wouldn't it? There's a Mel Brooks showing in town. You want to come tonight?"

"OK."

"You don't sound too enthusiastic about it."

"I'm sorry, Scott. Actually I don't feel like going anywhere or doing anything."

"I know how you feel, but come anyway."

I managed a weak smile. "OK, I will. Thanks."

The movie was just what we needed. It was silly, and it took our minds off our problems completely for a couple of hours. Afterward we went to have a soda, and by the time we drove home, the happy mood had gone again.

"I suppose I knew she would drop me in the end," Scott said. "She was always flirting. And she is so good-looking I suppose I didn't stand a chance ... she was too good for me."

"She was not!" I said hotly. "You're great

157

looking, too, and a great football player and—
and I think Angie was darned lucky that you
even noticed her!"

"Really?" he asked, a flicker of enthusiasm
crossing his face. "You think I'm OK?"

"You know I do."

"You know, I've always thought a lot of you,
too. I've always liked you since that day you
stood up to me and walked across that ledge.
That took a lot of guts. You're a great girl,
Joanna."

"Thanks."

For a while we drove on in silence. Then we
pulled up at my house.

"Joanna," Scott said hesitantly. "I've been
thinking. We've always gotten along together.
How about you and I going together? That
would show them, wouldn't it?"

Before I could stop him, he pulled me to
him and kissed me hard on the mouth. I
waited, but there were no bells ringing this
time. I was aware of the screech of crickets
outside the car and that I was waiting pa-
tiently for the kiss to end.

"It's no use, Scottie," I said at last. "I really
like you a lot. I've always wanted you for a
friend, but I only want Rick for a boyfriend. If
I can't have him, then I guess I'd rather have
no one."

"I understand," he said. "I suppose I feel the

same way about Angie. But thanks. You've made me feel a whole lot better, and we're going to stay friends, aren't we? After all, you wouldn't desert an old football buddy?"

That evening with Scott made me feel better, too. At least it showed me that I could get another boy if I wanted one. The one trouble was that I didn't want one. As I said to Scott, if I couldn't have Rick, I would rather retire to a convent.

The next morning I was summoned to Coach Parker's office. I had been expecting it. Rick had not shown up for practice all week, and, of course, I could hardly play in a doubles tournament if I didn't have a partner. So I was expecting the coach to tell me officially that Tony and Bill would be representing the school in the cup.

When I opened the door to Coach Parker's tiny broom-closet-sized office and squeezed inside, the first person I bumped into, literally, was Rick. He shrank against the wall as if I were carrying some terrible contagious disease. Coach Parker sat at his desk and scowled at both of us.

"All right, you two. It's time we did some serious talking," he said. "I gather that you had a fight. I gather that you are not speaking to each other. OK. Fair enough. What you do with your private lives is your own business, but you are both members of my tennis team. When you tried out for this team, you committed yourselves to the whole season. I told you already that I wanted to win the State Cup this year. I still aim to win it. If I play Tony and Bill, I have no chance of doing that. Anyway, why should I play Tony and Bill when I have two top-rated players? So I'm telling you right now: you need not like each other; you need not speak to each other if you don't want to. But next Saturday you are going to get out on that court and play together. And what's more, you are going to play to win. If you don't do that, I'll make sure you are finished in the tennis world, believe me. Both of you. I know all the coaches who matter. I recommend for scholarships, and I call in talent scouts when I think I have something worth seeing. If you don't play on Saturday, you don't ever play again. Do I make myself clear? Now, get out, both of you."

We went our separate ways, without a glance at each other.

Chapter Sixteen

I had been dreading Saturday, wondering if I could make myself sick, wondering how I would make it through the day, let alone win. But when our bus pulled up in the parking lot and I saw all the other school buses, row upon row of them like a giant beehive, it really hit me for the first time. "Wow! This is big stuff!" I couldn't help feeling excited.

When I saw the bleachers filled with all those strange faces, I began to feel more than excited. I began to feel nervous.

"We don't have to play our first matches in front of all those people, do we?" I asked Coach Parker when Rick was out of hearing.

"It all depends on the draw. One first round and one second round are played on that court, then two quarter-finals, both semis and, of course, the final. Why don't we go in and

161

check you in right now? Then you can see where you're going to be playing."

He walked with me over to the steward, who checked us off and handed us a time schedule and a plan of all the courts.

"You're in luck," Coach said. "Your first match is not on the main court. It's way out in the boondocks. Now go and change and meet me right here in ten minutes."

At least I had one thing to be glad about. If we lost our first-round match, nobody would see us losing.

The place where the tournament was held every year was an expensive private club. I found my way to the ladies' locker room. It was positively luxurious—carpeted in pale blue with gold-edged mirrors. It was only then, as I sat down all alone to put on my tennis shoes, that I realized all the other competitors would be boys. I had gotten so used to playing with Rick, Tony, and Bill that I didn't think there was anything unusual about it. But I soon found out it was unusual enough to be noticed by a whole lot of people this morning.

The first hint came when I had just about finished getting ready. A woman spectator came in to use the bathroom. When she saw me, dressed in my tennis outfit, she stopped me. "I'm sorry, honey, but you won't get any play today. Didn't they tell you there's a big tournament going on?"

I nodded. "Yes. I'm part of it."

"Oh—but I thought it was only for boys," she said.

I gave my hair a final, quick brush and picked up my rackets. "Actually, I'm really a boy," I said. "I just came in here for some peace and quiet, it's so crowded in the other dressing room." Then I walked out feeling much better already.

As yet Rick and I still hadn't said a word to each other. All the way down in the bus, we had sat as far apart as possible and deliberately stared out of opposite windows. But now, at last, the moment had come when we had to play tennis together. I walked down to where Coach Parker was waiting. Rick was already there, staring at some people already warming up on a court. "Ah, good, here's Joanna," Coach said.

Rick didn't even turn around. "OK, pay attention, you two," Coach went on. "Your first match is on court five. You go down through those trees and to your right. Now this match is an easy draw for you. You'll be playing Benjamin Franklin High from Charlestown. It's only a small school, and they shouldn't have too many good players. But if you get through that round, you meet one of the toughest teams in the competition. East Side from Boston. They lost the cup last year in a tie breaker, and this year you can bet they are determined to win it back. Now go over and warm up. And remember: play as a team, understand?"

"Yes, Coach," we both muttered. We walked down the tree-lined path toward the court. The silence between us became unbearable. In the end I had to say something. Trying to make my voice sound cool, calm, and indifferent, I said, "Look, whatever we feel about each other, it shouldn't affect the way we play today. Just forget you are playing with me, and let's try to win, OK?"

"Fine," he said, and for a fraction of a second his eyes met mine before he looked away.

The two boys from the other team were already on the court. They looked up with amused faces as we approached.

"Is this the team from Oakview High?"

"That's us."

They looked at each other with open delight.

"You always have a girl playing on your team?" one of them asked Rick. "Aren't there enough boys at your school?"

"You wait till you see her play," Rick said. "Then you won't be smiling."

I shot him a grateful glance. He could have said something horrible about me, but he had defended me.

We took our places on the court. I was determined to play extra well to make those Franklin boys eat their words. Rick looked at me. He could tell from the thwack of the first ball I sent across that I meant business. Actually, when the game started, we didn't even need the psychological boost of my being a girl. They were not nearly as good as we were, and it only took thirty-five minutes to win our two sets against them.

On the way back from that court, we still didn't speak to each other. Matches were still going on all around us, and from different parts of the club, you could hear cheers, sighs, or applause. We had enough time to sip a cool drink and sit down and watch our next opponents. They were in the middle of a tough match against Huntington Park, whose number one had been my first and greatest conquest. Huntington was making them fight for every point and in the end, when East Side was finally victorious, Rick turned to me and said in a whisper, "I bet what's-his-name from Huntington would be pleased to know he has just helped us by wearing out our opponents for us."

Then he realized he had spoken to me, and he frowned and moved away.

Even though the East Side boys had been playing for an hour, they were clearly not going to be worn out, or easy to beat. They were both big, tough-looking boys, and they seemed full of energy after a brief rest. Unlike the Franklin team we had just creamed, they showed almost no surprise at having to play me, which made them rise even higher in my estimation.

Then we started to play, and I forgot that I was playing with Rick or that I was playing against one of the top-seeded teams. My one aim was to win. Their style of tennis was not like Rick's and mine. They didn't rush in to attack. They stayed on the base line and returned everything, waiting for their opponents to make an error. They were infuriating to play, reaching unreachable smashes, lobbing over our heads when we came up to net, and generally seeming to have arms a mile long. Like Huntington Park before us, we found ourselves fighting for every point, thinking we had it won, only to see the ball come flying back at us once again. At five-all in the first set, we were holding our own, but it was beginning to tell on our nerves.

Then, in the vital eleventh game, Rick hit a smash not quite as hard as he had intended. It landed at their feet and was whipped back, right between us and straight down the center line. Rick and I turned to each other angrily. "That was your ball!" we both yelled at the same time.

For a moment nobody moved. Then, as we looked at each other, our mouths began to twitch, the twitch became a smirk, the smirk a chuckle, and with a great burst of laughter we fell into each other's arms. We laughed and laughed and laughed. Then, when the laughter died down, Rick kissed me fondly as if we were alone in the middle of a forest and not with a million or so people watching.

"I've missed you so much," he whispered. "I've been a stubborn idiot."

"I've missed you, too."

"Do you forgive me?"

"It was as much my fault as yours."

"Did I ever tell you that Angie Peterson is boring?"

"Hey, you two," came a growl from the other side of the court. "How long are we expected to stand here and watch young love in the spring? Or is that part of your tactics to make us lose concentration?"

"Yes, Oakview, please resume play immediately," said the umpire in his flat voice.

Rick looked at me. "Are you ready to start playing again?"

I nodded.

"OK, let's go get 'em, shall we?" he said, winking.

"You bet," I said as I walked back to serve.

About an hour later, Rick and I had the double pleasure of watching the final score posted (we had won, 7-5, 6-4, and 6-2), while we sat holding hands and graciously accepting the congratulations of our friends. Finally, when everyone had cleared out, Rick gave me a sort of "OK, now that we're alone" kind of look and said, "Joanna, if we hadn't made up, do you think we still would have beaten those guys?"

I thought for a moment. I knew deep down, even though I was glad we had made up, that when I'm on that court, absolutely nothing interferes with my playing. Not even Rick. I decided, however, that our truce was too fragile for brutal honesty. So I put on what I hoped was my best "Scarlett O'Hara, Southern belle" kind of voice and said very sweetly, "Oh, Rick, you know I always play as hard as I can, but it was wonderful having a really together partner, even if he was a boy!"

And before Rick could have time to react, I quickly kissed him on the cheek and ran, as fast as I could, into the ladies' locker room.

**If you enjoyed this book, read
these great new Sweet Dreams romances.**

COVER GIRL by Yvonne Green

Overnight Renée has become a glamorous high
fashion model. But she's hiding her new life
from her boyfriend Greg—who loves Renée for
what she used to be. Once he finds out the
truth, will he ever trust her again?

LOVE MATCH by Janet Quin-Harkin

When Joanna joins the boys' tennis team and
meets Rick, she finds love for the first time.
But Rick's the #1 player on the team...or at
least he was until Joanna came along. Can
they both play to win without losing each other?

THE PROBLEM WITH LOVE
by Susan Mendonca

Cathy's the partying type. John's the serious
type. But when her parents hire John as her
math tutor, Cathy suddenly gets very serious.
Because for once, the funny girl is in love.

NIGHT OF THE PROM
by Debra Spector

Barbara's the hardest working editor the school
paper has ever had. But is she missing out on
all the fun? When Michael dares her to trade
her typewriter for a prom gown, Barbara finally
gets the inside scoop on romance.